★

I was halfway to Pyrite Junction on 73, going through the curves where the hillside comes down nearly sheer on the left, and the right shoulder drops off ten feet into the creek bed, when a black, chopped-down Harley with the customary bad mufflers came up behind me. I heard the bike accelerate to pass. He stayed alongside me too long. I looked left to see why and got a head-on view of a sawed-off shotgun barrel.

I dove to the right, flat as I could get on the seat. I couldn't hit the brake in that position, but my foot came off the gas when I started to move and slowed the truck enough to put the blast into my fender more than my door. The Harley took off.

★

ALEC KALLA & M. J. SULLIVAN

Velvet

WORLDWIDE.

TORONTO • NEW YORK • LONDON
AMSTERDAM • PARIS • SYDNEY • HAMBURG
STOCKHOLM • ATHENS • TOKYO • MILAN
MADRID • WARSAW • BUDAPEST • AUCKLAND

For CMSgt. Richard C. Capps, USAF (ret.),
and his wife, Jean.

One meets so few grande dames in this life.
We have been privileged to know one.

To you, Jean Chamberlin.

VELVET

A Worldwide Mystery/April 2005

First published by Foul Play Press.

ISBN 0-373-26526-3

Printed in U.S.A.

Acknowledgments

Grateful acknowledgment is extended to
Dr. Diane McHose and Sifu Donn Hayes
for their advice on medical matters relevant to
the book. Any errors remaining are entirely
the fault of the authors. We would also like
to thank Lou Kannenstine of Foul Play Press,
copy editor Larry Hamberlin, and to extend
special thanks to Richard Hill, who put us all in touch.

ONE

IT'S NOT DREAD of the menace from the east—I like the rising sun—it's just that I like to drift up peacefully from the darkness, listening to the birds singing and the dawn wind rushing through the pines, the mountain sunrise reflecting off the clouds and from my ceiling. I hate being jerked awake when some fool rings my telephone at daybreak. I shouldn't even have a phone. Maybe someday I can afford the luxury.

I threw off the blankets and stomped across the sleeping loft to Ma Bell's instrument of torture and sat down at my desk. The cold of the wooden chair came through my jockeys immediately. I keep the cabin windows open.

"This better be good," I growled into the receiver.

"Hank? Hank, this is Sue." She was sobbing.

This was not how I wanted to begin my first day off in weeks. I'd been hard at it, patching barbed-wire fences on the ranch and getting it ready for the cattle that would ship in on the first of June for summer grazing. In the meantime, I had been trying to earn enough at odd jobs to keep from depleting my meager bank account.

"Yeah, Sue. What's going on?" I wasn't up for being the understanding shoulder to a space cadet ex-flame that had burned out years ago. I was her handyman now.

"Hank, can you come over? Right now? I'm...I need..." Shakey voice, more sobbing.

"What's broken?"

"Nothing. Nothing's broken, but Bill's not..."

I thumbed mentally through the list of Sue's male friends to Bill, her most recent live-in. I remembered he had the same light brown hair and blue eyes that I do. Sue was consistent. He was half a foot shorter than me, though. Five-six, maybe. That's as far as I went. If I wake up in danger, I wake up fast and deal with it. If not, my mind goes back to sleep until I brew some brains in the coffee pot. No one was kicking in the door, and the only animals outside were two elk, who had graciously spent the winter consuming half my horses' hay rations. I watched through my window as they chowed down on my second attempt to get a summer vegetable supply started. A late frost got the first try. I waited for Sue to get hold of herself and tell me what she wanted to wheedle me into this time.

"What about Bill?" I prompted.

"I think he's dead." Flat and sotto voce. I woke up.

"Dead? Are you sure?"

"Yes. No. I mean, please, can't you come over? Right away? Please, Hank. I don't know who else to call and I need someone here."

Sucker that I am. "All right, Sue. Did you call the sheriff yet?"

"No."

"Then do It. Now. I'll be over."

I hung up and climbed down from the loft, let the dog out to bark and chase the elk out of the garden, and put some water in the kettle for coffee. I made a quick stab at washing my face and brushing my teeth, then dressed in the jeans and boots I'd worn yesterday. I didn't want to waste time swapping my belt and pocket contents. I put on a clean shirt and gulped a cup of lukewarm instant Folger's.

The morning was sharp and clean, with lazy rose clouds in a robin's-egg sky. A perfect late spring day in the Colorado foothills. It was pushing June, and the last serious snow except maybe one was past. It would have been a nice day to go for a walk and relax, but someone had, as usual, screwed it up by dragging me into something I didn't have to be in, laying a claim on friendship and humanity. If I was the grouch so many people think I am I could enjoy my spring mornings.

Musashi had chased the elk out and was finishing his morning toilet, sniffing the wind. A good dog, an Akita. Handsome, gentle, and trained enough to follow a command when necessary. True enough to his ancestry not to be blindly obedient. Spoiled and loved enough to get away with it. I called him in, locked up, and headed for Sue's place in Cottonwood.

It's twenty miles north from my house to town, half of it on a twisting, two-lane asphalt road, but you learn a piece of road over the years. It's posted at thirty. With no traffic and no troopers my record is twenty-five minutes, but a pickup truck is no Ferrari and Highway 73 no race-track. Pine trees make lousy hood ornaments. I took it easy so I could be wide awake as well as alive when I got to Sue's.

I thought about Sue as I was driving, wondering how I'd once felt so much and now felt so little. I'd known her about four years. We'd met at a Christmas party, but I can't remember whose. She was attractive enough, average height, a little thin but not a fashion model. Her strawberry blond hair hanging past her shoulders and the blue eyes that belong with it combined with enough girlishness to make me stumble afoot for her faster and maybe a little farther than she did for me.

It didn't end, it just changed. I like sex with candles and incense as well as the next guy, but dreamy exclamations about planetary influences at the critical moment get old in a hurry. I became a sort of uncle to her, fixed her broken plumbing, and tried on occasion to suggest she pay a little attention to the real work now and then. Something we all need to do.

Cottonwoods line the road along the creek the last mile before town, giving the place its name. For a couple of weeks in autumn they form a golden pavilion, but they were springtime yellow-green now, greedy for life. Beautiful in a different way, but at odds with the morning's errand.

Sue lived on Piñon Trail, a little dead-end uphill of the main street in town. You get a good look at the lake on the way up. The dam was built in the twenties, for flood control and to spur a shift from logging and cattle to summer resorts. It succeeded part way, and in the late sixties developers started pushing Cottonwood toward a bedroom community for Denver. I arrived in the seventies, somewhere between ten and a hundred years late for the heyday of the lifestyle I chose. The area is still changing, but there's room for a lot of different styles.

Sue's is a stone house converted in the seventies from someone's forties summertime retreat into a year-round rental by sticking city water on one side and a propane furnace on the other. In the seventies you could rent out a goat shed around here. You still can until someone turns you in to the county.

When I got there, the ambulance had arrived and was parked with its lights off. Not a good sign. The driver and an attendant were standing around outside. That meant they were waiting for the coroner and the sheriff. I considered ducking out of there and saving myself a lot of trouble, but I'd given my word to Sue, and then a deputy pulled in right behind me. I killed the engine and got out.

Right off I knew I didn't want to be there. The ambulance personnel were staring at me, burning my identity into their memories. I could sense the deputy behind me, making sure I didn't get away.

"I'm a friend of Sue Fenton's," I said. "What happened?" The eyes in front kept staring. Part of their EMT training I guess, facial expressions and how to inflict them.

"A friend, huh?" From behind me. I hate that. It feels like a scene out of a cheap western.

I turned around slow, following the script. The deputy was young, dark hair and a mustache, small frame and a cocky expression. I hadn't seen this one before, but the turnover rate among Madison County deputies is exceeded only by the checkout rate of best-sellers at the library. I don't know if it's bad pay and boredom or the color of the uniforms, forest-green shirts and gold trousers. They look pretty much alike, anyway, male or female. The cocky expression.

"Hi, officer. My name is Hank Eston. I just got here."

I stopped. I didn't want to run on at the mouth. He just looked at me blankly. That meant expectantly. Too much silence wouldn't do either.

"Sue called me, upset, and I told her to call you. I got here as soon as I could. What happened?"

Tactful small talk isn't my strong point, so I did my best "golly shucks" routine. It doesn't do to act too much out of character because word choices always give away a college education. Still, people expect anyone with cow shit on their boots to have horse shit in their brains, and dealing with the Sheriff's Department over the years with fence line disputes and estrays, I'd found it worked best. Usually.

"Suppose you tell me," he said. Out came a notepad and pencil.

"Sue said she thought her boyfriend had died and asked me to come over. I came."

"Uh-huh. Back up a minute. Give me your name, address, and phone number."

I gave it to him, with the PO box.

"You got a street number, or do you live in a mailbox?"

I'd heard that line, word for word, from every official with a paper to shuffle in the last ten years. They wanted street numbers continuing out from Denver. I don't want to live in Denver, and the system meant places like the ranch would have seven-digit numbers out on the highway, where a mailbox isn't safe and where no one would be able to use them to locate anything anyway. It doesn't affect me much, really, but it strips away my sense of being safely, privately nestled in the hills. Maybe it's just my way of tilting against real estate development in the area. Maybe I'm trying to recapture the enchantment I felt as a boy wandering alone through empty hollows in West Virginia before my family lost our first farm. Friends laugh at my monomania, but it rankles, somehow. Besides, there's no law about it, and a person ought to exercise freedom every chance he gets, to keep it alive.

I said, "No. I live in a street number." So much for golly shucks.

"Boy, you got an attitude, you know that? I've got half an idea to take it out of you, right now. Give me an address before I put cuffs on you."

I wasn't impressed by it, but I didn't miss the stab at intimidating me. I had six inches on this rooster, but then he had the county and the cuffs. I compromised, something I'm not overly fond of doing.

"Are you familiar with the Pyrite Junction area?" I asked.

"Just give me a street address. What's the big deal here?"

We kept our eyes locked, both pissed and holding our ground. "I live eleven miles south, two miles off the highway, north side, up Wapiti Creek. The last place on the road."

"You the guy with the firewood sign by the gate?" he asked.

"Yeah, that's me."

"Why do you have a firewood sign two miles off the highway?" he asked.

That brought me up short and I finally had to acknowledge my lack of interest in being a businessman, even small scale.

"I guess I don't really want to sell much firewood."

He looked down at his pad and wrote something.

"Okay. I'll let it go for now. When did Miss Fenton call you?"

"Dawn."

"What time was it?"

"I didn't look at a clock, but the sky was still red."

"Give me a time, will you?"

I thought I had. "What time is it now?" I asked.

"Seven-thirty."

I thought a second. "Then I guess it'd be around six-thirty or so when she called."

"About six-thirty?"

"Yeah."

"And what was your relation to the deceased?"

"Deceased? He's dead then?"

"That's what I said. How well did you know him?"

Shit. Too late now. "I didn't. I do repair work for Sue. I never really talked to Bill, just saw him a couple times at a party or when I was working here."

"Then why are you here now? Why did Miss Fenton call you?"

"I don't know," I said. "I wish to hell she hadn't, right about now."

"I bet you do. We're not done yet. Let's see a driver's license."

I reached for my wallet, a little too fast, I guess, because the deputy's hand started toward his right hip. I slowed way up. I'd forgotten that something about me can make people nervous. I showed him my license. He wrote the number down, checked my face against the picture, and grunted.

"Okay. Stick around."

"Can I talk to Sue?" He studied me a moment, decided I was more a pain in the ass than a danger.

"Yeah," he shrugged. "Come along with me, but don't touch anything and don't get in the way."

It didn't seem like missing breakfast had helped my social graces, but then not much does.

I followed him up the outside stairs and through the open front door. Sue was inside, next to a female ambulance attendant, leaning against a long wall decorated with odd charts and paintings and the ubiquitous aloe plant. She had her fists stuck as far into her mouth as they'd go and her eyes were wide. She was sobbing gently, tears wetting her cheeks. When she saw me she ran over and put her arms around me.

"Oh! I'm so glad you came. Thank you," she sniffed.

"Miss, are you Sue Fenton?" He had his job to do, filling up notebook pages.

While the deputy was questioning Sue a good-looking brunette woman, mid-twenties, showed up carrying a Gladstone bag. An assistant coroner for Madison County, and overdressed for the occasion. Overdressed for the area anytime, in my opinion, but to balance things out, the rocks in the driveway had claimed one of her high heels. She walked with an enforced limp and a look of annoyance on her face. Someone forgot to tell her that some of the county hasn't been paved yet.

"Where is it?" she demanded, looking from Sue to the deputy to me. Lots of compassion in her today.

"He's over there, on the couch." The ambulance attendant pointed.

"Okay. Let's have a look." She opened her satchel and removed two thermometers, put one on the sofa, and checked the temperature of the body with the other.

"What's the story?" she asked. We all looked at Sue.

"Go ahead, tell her," I said.

"Well, I woke up and he wouldn't wake up and I tried to shake him and he didn't, I mean he wouldn't…I called Hank and then he said, 'Call the ambulance,' so I did and then you came."

"What time did you get up?" the coroner asked.

"It was around six-thirty, I think, 'cause the colors were just spreading across my door there and that happens—''

''Colors?'' asked the deputy.

Sue tossed her hair back and said, ''Yeah. See, I have a crystal prism hanging in my window, by the bed, to direct the actinic rays.''

''Actinic rays. I see.'' The deputy looked disgusted. He and I agree on something at least.

The coroner uncovered the entire body. He was wearing a silver crucifix. There were a few small cuts on his face, but nothing that looked to me bad enough to have killed him. She pressed on his cheek. It remained white.

''Turn him over, would you?'' she said to the EMT guys.

They did. There were three pretty good bruises, one on his left shoulder, one on the right thigh, and a nasty one just above his right hip. The last one was swollen. I thought about the last good bump I'd taken. How long had it taken to turn yellow around the edges?

''How did he receive these injuries?'' asked the coroner. ''They can't be more than twelve hours old.''

''Do you know?'' asked the deputy, looking at Sue.

Having something to do and people to do it with

was helping Sue a little. The pace of her speech didn't slow, but the tone calmed down.

"Well, he came home last night all beat up, and I asked him, 'What happened to you?' and he said, 'Nothing, I'm okay,' but I could see he wasn't so I sat him down on the sofa there and I could see he was stiff and everything so I went and got some water and a towel and started cleaning him up and helping him and he was groaning and everything so I said, 'Damn it, what can I do for you? How about a massage?' I'm a massage therapist, you know, and he said, 'Fine. Sure. Give me a massage and a drink, too.' So I made him a whiskey like he likes and, well, I got him to lay down and I worked on his liver meridians mainly, he usually needed that, and he started talking a little. 'You wouldn't believe it,' he said and I said, 'What,' and he said 'Those creeps. I told the guys I was quitting and they just beat me up.' I got him another drink and he kept telling about what happened and I—"

"Miss Fenton? Excuse me, please," said the deputy. I wanted to thank him for interrupting. "Where did Bill work?"

"Gee, you know, I don't really know why he came home when he did, it was about ten. He works nights as a mechanic at the freight office, you know,

the trucking company on the north end of town, but
why would they beat him up for quitting?''

"I don't know," said the deputy. "Did he say
anything about that?"

"No."

"Do you know why he quit?"

Sue's verbal landslide stopped. She looked at the
floor for a few seconds. She didn't look up when
she spoke.

"No."

She stopped, biting her lip.

We were saved by the arrival of more deputies
with cameras, fingerprint kits, and all the parapher-
nalia of an investigation. It seemed pretty obvious
that Bill hadn't died of natural causes. Sue and I
got free limousine service to the county seat in Silvern, chauffeured by the Sheriff's Department.

TWO

EVEN WHEN YOU'RE innocent and only there for questioning, the Madison County jail has a way of disturbing your peace of mind, as if you're on your way to Stalin's salt mines. Sue and I were kept apart from the time we left her house in sheriff's custody. I was escorted through the front door—known bad guys go handcuffed through the back—because appearances of civility are helpful up to a point. I don't know what became of Sue.

I traded my driver's license for a black pass at the front desk. They hold it for ransom, I guess. I noticed the guy next to me turning in a green pass labeled "visitor" on his way out. At least they didn't suit me up in orange prisoner fatigues. They did put my pocket knife with my license, though.

"You can claim this when you leave," the desk clerk said. He eyed my belt, really wanting to take it. It put things in perspective.

A deputy escorted me down a hall that was just

narrow enough to make me claustrophobic. It looked twice as long as the building, but that had to be a trick of prison architecture.

"This way please. In here please." I stepped inside and heard the door lock behind me. A nice melodramatic touch, the door with a noisy dead bolt. Trapped and alone. Wondering what happens now. They left me to stew and think and sweat awhile.

Innocent, nothing to worry about, right? Except that an ex-flame's live-in boyfriend who's half my size gets beaten to death and the ex-flame called me first and I showed up at the death scene. As a cop, would I be thinking jealousy, triangle? There were lawyers' bills ahead, almost for sure.

I recognize the necessity of government and police. Not everyone in this world is reasonable and responsible. But a number of things in my family history make me touchy about officials twisting the rules for expediency, and being locked inside the jailhouse didn't help my attitude at all. I made a conscious effort to relax by studying the room I was in.

It was institutional green, twelve by twelve. Dirty linoleum. Cheap perforated acoustic tile on the walls and ceiling, maybe concealing mikes and cameras. One brown metal folding chair for the suspect, two padded chairs, and a table. Popcorn crumbs on the floor and the stench of stale urine. These guys must work on people, laughing and eating popcorn while some poor bastard is sitting here pissing all over himself.

The door pushed open and Torquemada walked in carrying a folder of papers.

"Riley," he said.

"Hank Eston," I said.

He was a caricature of the New York, Italian police detective, round, balding, sleeves rolled up hairy arms, an empty shoulder holster, food stains on his shirt and loosened tie. Tired lines around his eyes suggested he was just doing a job and waiting for his pension.

"Riley?" I asked incredulously.

"So someone at Ellis Island had a sense of humor when my family went through. Sit down. What are you doing here?"

"You know better than I do. I don't know beans about this."

He shot me a look, then opened the file.

"We ran you through the NCIC computer. It says you're clean. Your prints are on the way from DC."

"Really?" I wasn't worried about a record turning up. I was surprised the Sheriff's Department was that efficient, though I knew Washington had my prints. I'd given up my chance at a life of crime when I'd traded them for a cab driver's license to get myself through college.

"Yeah, wiseass. We can move when we feel like it." He looked at his papers. "Thirty-five. Self-employed. No money, unless you cheat like crazy on your taxes. Registered Independent. So you got absolutely no clout around here, right?"

Then, in a bad imitation of a Southern smokey, with no smile at all, he said, "Boy, you in a heap o' trouble."

I tried to figure out first how they gathered all that personal information so quickly. Did they keep a KGB dossier on everyone in the county? And then I wondered how I'd managed to tick him off so fast. I guessed it was from past encounters with the department, when I'd stepped on some politically connected toes on the subject of fence lines. It could just have been his standard interrogation routine. Or maybe he'd gotten a recommendation from the officer on the scene. I should have had something for breakfast.

"Why'd you beat up Bill Evans?" he demanded. "You and Sue got something going?"

"I didn't, and no, we don't. I quit running after her years ago. We're just friends."

"Do you ride?"

"Yeah."

"What do you got? What kind?"

"Arab-quarter horse mix. A mare and a gelding. Both sorrels."

"I mean motorcycles. You got one?"

"Why motorcycles?" I asked.

"Just answer the question."

"No, I've never owned one."

Riley shrugged.

"Look," I said, "I'm willing to help if I can, but mostly I just want to get the heck out of here. I left a large dog in a small house and he's going to need to go out. Can I make a phone call sometime?"

"Sure, sure. Soon's we're done here. If you don't know nothing and you ain't so close to this girl how come she's calling you first thing, huh?"

"I don't know. Maybe she thinks because I fix her sink I'm the one to solve all her problems."

I got that far when the door opened again, a little less dramatically, and a serene-looking Japanese man leaned in. Business suit and a half smile to Riley.

"How is it going?" he asked of Riley.

"Just fine. I'll talk with you when I'm done here, Takayama."

Takayama nodded. He looked at me as if I was

a curio left on the table by mistake. He had the inscrutable Oriental role down as well as Riley had the tough Dago cop. I suppose it could be as effective as hell on some people, but it was beginning to annoy me.

"DA's office," Riley explained when the Japanese left. "Look. I'll tell you what. I want to believe you, not a hundred percent maybe, but I want to. Shit happens and sometimes a nice guy just gets stuck in it. An accident. So listen. Let's talk a little more and maybe then you go home. Okay? Okay."

"Thanks," I said.

"Hey, no thanks needed. So what do you do up there in the hills? I mean, you're self-employed, but what do you do? Construction? Yeah. You said you're a handyman, didn't you?"

"Yeah, and some firewood. I look after some grazing land, run a few head of cattle. I get by."

"Whose land? You don't own it."

"My uncle does. He bought it and tried living out here for a while, but his wife hated it. They don't even come out summers anymore."

"Yeah, sure. You're batchin' it, ain't you? What do you do for kicks? You hunt? Fish? Get stoned?"

I gave a short laugh. "I hunt a little, fish a little. Read and play a little music. Lots of walks and as little work as I can get away with. Occasionally I'll drink a beer and chase the women around."

"Yeah, sure. Where were you yesterday? Tell me your day."

I told him.

"What about the nighttime?"

"I ate dinner and took a bath. Then I read until I went to sleep."

"What'd you read?"

"I don't know. Wait a minute, yes I do. I re-read some Sherlock Holmes stories."

"Which ones?"

"Is this important?" I asked.

"Let me ask, you answer. Which ones?"

I told him. He asked me for the plots. I knew all the Holmes stories nearly by heart. I told him that, too. He shrugged.

"Can anyone prove you were home last night? All night?"

I thought about it. Did anyone phone? No. No one came to visit. My turn to shrug.

"Just my dog."

Riley wasn't amused.

"Listen, you're right. There's nothing concrete on you. Yet. I'm going to take a chance on you, but you know how this looks. Get out of here. Go home and try to remember something that proves where you were last night, but don't leave town. And you keep your nose out of this from now on. One more thing. I'll be watching out for you, okay?"

"Okay," I said. "When can I see Sue?"

"Some other time. Now get out of here."

"How do I get home? My truck's in Cottonwood."

"Hey, what do I look like, a taxi dispatch? Get out of here."

GREAT. IT WAS AFTER three o'clock and I had better than twenty miles to go with no food in me. I don't want to be of service to my government too often.

Hitchhiking is as illegal in Colorado as loitering, so I walked toward the southwest end of town to catch the highway. At the top of Washington Street I checked my wallet for cash and splurged on a burger and coffee at the Sonic burger stand, to go, so I could keep moving. I wanted to time my arrival at the highway to match my hitchhiking with the rush hour and minimize my chances of getting a ticket. The rush hour I was concerned about is four-thirty to four-fifty, when all the sheriff's cars have rushed into Silvern for the shift change. The sheriff must have it set up so no one commits a crime for those twenty minutes. It wouldn't be cricket. From what I'd seen of the Sheriff's Department, it was possible that most of the criminals in the county were in Silvern for that period.

I walked south on Highway 6 until the flow of Madison County patrols quit, then stuck out my thumb. Hitching, when you're a kid and smiling, isn't too hard. When you look over thirty and grumpy as hell, people tend to pass you by, wondering why you're not driving your own Mercedes. I kept walking. It wouldn't be the first time I'd walked twenty miles, but it wouldn't be fun. Unlike professional joggers who favor ninety-dollar sweatpants and hundred-dollar sneakers, I was wearing my usual jeans and five pounds of western boots. And I've never developed a real taste for exhaust fumes. Just a man out of my time.

I was going up the hill to I-70 when a jeep pulled over and gave me a ride. I thanked the driver even before I told him I was headed to Cottonwood. He was, too.

We went under the interstate and down Colorado 93, just west of the hogback, a crenellated upthrust of several million years of sandstone serving as a last redoubt against overcrowding and cheap condos development. To the east, on the flats, you can bulldoze the plains and put in the street signs. West of the hogback you generally need dynamite and a lot more money. You don't necessarily get better people, just fewer of them.

The hills there are sparsely covered with buckbrush and grass, letting the red of the sandstone soil show through, and downhill toward the town of Morrison the bare stone slabs of the Red Rocks area tilt up to make a giant's playground. We went west up rocky Bear Creek Canyon, one of the prettiest places there is when someone else is watching for oncoming traffic on the wrong side of blind curves. The drivers around here get worse each year.

I got out on Cottonwood's main street and thanked my ride. Ordinarily I can appreciate the beauty of the snow-capped peaks beyond the green hills that surround Cottonwood, but I was slightly numb from the wind buffeting and engine roar in the open jeep, and from the whole day's events. Mostly what registered in my mind was the rudeness of the commuters coming up from Denver, rushing to get home in their Audis and Mercedes. I missed the old days when the town hadn't needed a traffic light and you could still hear the foaming of Bear Creek's water roiling downstream across the boulders. But I had enough to think about without trying to arbitrate aesthetics. I walked to Sue's, got in my truck and drove home.

When I reached my front fence I knew someone

was on the property. The gate wasn't chained shut the way I do it. There were two sets of tire tracks in the dirt road, but two different sets. That meant they were still on the place. I drove on in to the house and found two sheriff's jeeps and four deputies outside the door. Musashi was raising hell.

"We could have gone in, you know," the deputy in charge said. "We have a warrant, but Riley said you're cooperating, so we thought we'd wait and enjoy the scenery. Sorry, but you'll have to stay outside while we search the place. Okay with you?"

"Do I have a choice?" I laughed and grinned. "Sure. Can I let my dog out first? I'll put him on the chain over there."

"All right," he said.

"Is there anything in particular you're looking for? Maybe I can save you some time. Maybe you could tell me why you're searching at all?"

He just smiled. "Want to read the warrant?"

"No. Have at it."

"All right. Get your dog and let's get this over with."

I brought out the Moose.

"What kind of mutt is that?" one of the other deputies asked as Musashi sniffed him. "I've never seen one of these before."

"He's an Akita, Japanese breed," I said. Moose is a hundred-plus pounds of adolescent affection, slobber, and bladder. He demonstrated all three before I chained him up.

I sat in a canvas chair on the porch. One of the deputies stood nearby, leaning on the rail, looking over my private refuge while his buddies searched the cabin. The valley is peaceful, green and moist in the spring. Framed on either side by slopes of tall pines, it draws the vision up through layers of forested hills to the rugged back slope of Pike's Peak. The peak itself stares back like a mystical eye.

"Nice place you got here," he said. "It reminds me of a fishing shack I used to go to in Wyoming. Too bad you got no stream close by."

"There used to be one. You can see the gully over there." I pointed to the east, about fifty yards away. "It quit running a few years ago when they drilled all the wells for the subdivision across the road. That happens a lot up here."

"Yeah. Still a nice view. I'd cut down some of those trees there so I had a clearer view of the mountains."

You'd pave the road and put up a street light, too. Everyone wants to live in the mountains. They just don't want them to be the mountains.

"A little too quiet and far off the road for me. What do you do when it snows? Don't you get stuck back here?"

"It's not that bad," I said. "You see the plow on the truck. Maybe three times a winter, if I forget to park at the top of the hill, the truck stays put for a day or two until the snow melts off. Or else I chain up and shovel the hill clear. Usually I put in the hubs on the truck and just plow out, then spend the day relaxing or cross-country skiing."

"Yeah. You got the life. My wife would never go for it, though." He shook his head.

"Perks of bachelorhood," I said.

They searched thoroughly but considerately, for cops, putting things back near where they were. It took me three hours to reshelve everything. They didn't find whatever they were looking for, but I knew they wouldn't. I wasn't hiding anything.

When they left I let the dog loose and we played fetch for a while. He was glad to see me home. He'd spent a hard day trying to digest two volumes of Kipling I'd left on the kitchen table. Someday he'll get me trained to keep all my books up out of his reach. I washed my cleanest dirty dishes and made dinner, then sat down to think.

I had to admit I made a convenient suspect for the cops. Strong, single, outdoor type beats hell out of his rival for his old girlfriend. It was easy for the sheriff, and the Madison County sheriff's motto has always been "whatever works the easiest." If I left it up to them I could win an all-expense-paid trip to the state pen in Canon City. I had no alibi, but then they had no evidence against me. How could they? I didn't do it. I took the dog and went for a walk.

Living on several hundred acres in the eastern foothills of the Rockies means having your own private park to roam. Walking through it in the spring won't give you all the answers you need, but it sure calms you down and gives you perspective. Summer's short this high up, so the wildflowers try to look their best for the short growing season they have. The elk that forage here learn who is a danger and when. Today I wasn't, and I walked past them without causing more than casual scrutiny. It's nice to see them relaxed. It reminds me that I'm part of the scheme of things, too.

Riley might claim I had troubles, but by the time I got home I had decided to continue with my quiet life and let the Sheriff's Department solve its own problem. I hadn't done anything except try to comfort a friend in distress. Even Madison's cops would figure that out eventually. I made my plans for the next day's work and settled in for the night.

THREE

TUESDAY I WATCHED the dawn. Seeing the snow on the high peaks color blood red is one of the things that make living in the high country worthwhile. I don't get homegrown tomatoes, at least not many, but I get great scenery and, usually, quiet.

After breakfast I loaded the dog and a few tools into the truck and left for Pyrite Junction to pick up some bolts I needed to repair the cattle unloading chute. I figured Sue would call me when she wanted to talk. I was halfway to the hardware store when a county cop pulled me over. I got out, which he didn't like, but he didn't push the point.

"What's wrong?" I asked. I hadn't been speeding. I couldn't think of how I'd screwed up. I gave him my driver's license and my truck registration, my proof of insurance, and my proof of air pollution program compliance. So far you don't need to carry a passport and birth certificate to drive in Colorado, but they're working on that. You can never have too much paperwork.

Without speaking to me, the deputy returned to his car and radioed in my ID, checking for high crimes and misdemeanors. I petted the dog through the window. When fifteen minutes or so had gone by I walked back to the patrol car, turned around so the officer could see my back pockets didn't conceal anything and put my hands in them, then turned to face him. I did it casually, as if I was looking across the road at the trees. It's a little thing, but it takes a split second of anxiety out of someone else's life.

"Why's it taking so long?" I asked. "I ought to be clean."

"Maybe they forgot me," he said. "I'll check."

They had. I was clean. The deputy got out and walked me to my truck, handing back my papers.

"I stopped you because you have a dirty license plate, but I'm not going to write you up this time."

My face must have shown disbelief. I'd never heard of anyone being stopped for a dirty plate. I knew it was possible. There's got to be a law covering that, since there's one for everything else in this state, but my plate wasn't that dirty.

I said, "Let me get my canteen and I'll clean it."

He didn't say anything. I opened my truck and reached behind the seat, coming up slowly—I didn't want to give him any extra excitement—with a rag and the canteen of water, got out, and polished my rear license plate. Then I scrubbed the front one.

"You might do the turn light lenses, too," he suggested.

"Why not?" I said. I cleaned them. "Thanks, officer."

"No problem. Just doing my job."

Right.

I headed for Pyrite Junction, where 73 hits the state highway. A post office and a gas station that sells the barest mountain necessities are tucked into the corner there under a pyrite-laced rock face. I bought the bolts, then stopped at the Wilhelm Associates, Inc., insurance office.

"Good morning, Hank," Kate Wilhelm said when I opened the door.

"Hello, Kate. How are you? How'd you and Jack come out on the pups?" I asked. Musashi had had the pleasure of meeting the Wilhelms' female Akita when she was receiving company last fall.

"Oh, we made a killing on them," she said. "Let's do it again sometime, okay?"

"Sure. I'll check Moose's date book for openings." I was annoyed that she only commented on the money, not on how the puppies were or what type of homes they'd been placed in.

"Kate," I said, "let me pay my truck insurance.'' I pulled a folded, smudged envelope from my back pocket and my wallet from my front. Kate frowned. ''What's wrong?'' I asked.

''Don't you have a check? Cash is such a bother.''

''Yeah, I can write you a check if you want.'' I pulled a folded, tattered check from one section of my wallet and filled it out. The frown deepened. It must have been the folds.

''There you are and thank you,'' she said, handing me a receipt and a proof-of-insurance certificate to add to the paperwork in my wallet.

''Tell me something, Kate.'' She smiled. ''The notice with my bill said medical costs are up fourteen percent. Auto repair costs are up eleven percent, and court costs are up ten percent from last year.''

Her head nodded and she said, ''That's correct.''

''Then why are my insurance bills going up twenty per-cent per year?''

Kate shook her head and laughed. ''Who knows? We're certainly not doing it. We just sell the policies.''

I nodded at her, not really agreeing, but recognizing that getting at the source of a problem is usually damned near impossible.

"Um-hmm," I said. "Well, thanks, Kate. See you next time."

On the way home I was stopped again, but this time it was for an obstructed windshield. I argued that the stuff I keep on my dashboard, my fence pliers and chain saw files, my first aid kit and work gloves, didn't obstruct my view of anything except the dashboard. It didn't matter. I dumped everything on the passenger's side floor. Again no ticket, but the two stops had turned a twenty-minute drive into an hour and a half.

I put the rest of the day in on the loading chute and finishing off the south front fence. It gave me lots of opportunity to watch traffic on the highway. I counted twenty-five county patrols going past. Normally there'd be four or five in a whole day. Riley was sending me a message, or maybe he wanted me to feel secure. I didn't.

Next day, with the fences all done, I decided to take the dog to my vet in Cottonwood to get him his rabies shots. On the way I was pulled over for a roadside safety check.

"Come on," I told the officer, "this is getting out of hand."

"What is?" he asked straight-faced.

"Nothing," I said. "Nothing at all." He ran me through the drill of lights, brakes, exhaust system.

"Well now, you're all legal and safe."

"Tell the rest of the department that, will you?"

"Thank you for your cooperation," he said. He'd wasted damned near an hour of my time, and I had to reschedule my vet appointment to the next day.

I drove by Sue's, but she wasn't there. I put a note in her door saying I'd been by and to let me know if I could help her with any problems Bill's death had brought up. Then I went to the grocery store, bought some sliced ham and onion rolls, and ate lunch sitting in my truck. There was no sense wasting more of the day. I went back to the ranch.

MY NEW APPOINTMENT at Doc Summer's vet clinic was at 9 a.m. I'd been up late Wednesday night reading cheap fiction, trying to keep myself from thinking about Bill Evans's death. I failed and slept in late enough to miss breakfast again.

The Moose passed his physical in fine form and got his walking papers for another year. I put his new rabies tag in front of the other two on his collar and went into Cottonwood for a late breakfast at the Pines Cafe, where Sue waited tables part-time.

Every small town has a gathering place, and if it's got any class at all it'll be a coffee shop. The Pines's foundation, and probably some of the building's timbers, date back to the 1880s. The site was a general store then, serving miners and loggers. It turned cafe in the twenties, changing its products but not its social functions.

Sue wasn't working, but I ordered a pot of coffee and a cinnamon roll anyway. The Pines makes the best around. I tried to call Sue from the pay phone and got her answering machine, which reminded me to recycle my trash. I wanted to ask where I could drop off the mental garbage I was saddled with, but hung up instead. I hate talking to tape recorders.

Back at my table I drank my second cup of the day. On one of the adjoining tables was a morning Denver Post. One convenient thing about the Pines, someone always leaves the latest paper lying around. Coffee and a roll cost two bucks, but you save the cost of a paper. Cheap, yeah, but every nickel counts when you're trying to stay free. I reached over and grabbed it.

Bill's death was on page eight. Lots of things were more important to a growing metroplex like Denver. He'd lost out to the latest gasoline tax hike, which was supposed to repair and update all the roads that hadn't been repaired with the last increase that was going to get them all. And to the annexation by Morrison of all the surrounding land that looked to be good for taxable development. But he came in ahead of another economic forecast of good times, high prices, and fast bucks just as soon as the area land market turned around. Sometimes it seems people only live here in order to speculate in real estate.

SUSPICIOUS DEATH IN COTTONWOOD was the caption, and the article went on in four paragraphs to give the press release issued by the Sheriff's Department. Coroner's report not in, but bruises and death apparently from an assault.

Nothing new there, so I read the front page and the comics and left the paper for someone else. I ate my roll and emptied the coffeepot. I paid and walked outside, stretched, and started a leisurely walk down Main Street.

I walked east, past the southwestern art gallery, the upscale sportswear shops, and the bank, all fronted in pseudo-Bavarian or contemporary western style. Across the side street I mounted the raised boardwalk in front of the Buck Saloon, sparing a glance at the half dozen Harleys parked below on the street, where saddle horses would have looked more appropriate. The boardwalk continued past shops selling alpine kitsch, secondhand clothes, and real estate. I guess the Buck set the style for that block, all early frontier. During breaks in the traffic

I heard the creek in the cottonwoods beyond the parking lot across the street.

I had no definite plans for the day other than to pick up a few things as long as I was in town. A few books, maybe, and some saddle soap and neat's-foot oil for my tack at the ranch.

A couple of minutes later I saw Luke Sigilli. Luke is in his thirties and believes he's living in a Louis L'Amour novel. I'd seen him in the National Forest now and again, toting a six-gun and carbine, walking silently with slitted eyes to no visible purpose. Being in town without the artillery always makes him nervous and furtive, but that's where he spends most of his time, cadging coffee or cigarettes. He used to be a stuntman at the wild west show in Idaho Springs, but his brains got too scrambled on mushrooms or peyote to be trusted to use blanks in the staged shoot-outs. He can be a pest, but you never know what you'll learn by listening to him ramble. He was leaning against the store— front of Geist's Boots and Saddles, between the hanging wagon wheels that form the Os in "Boots," waiting for someone or something of interest to wander by.

"Hey, Luke, how's it going?" I asked when I got up to him. I hunkered down under the B. I never stand when I can sit and I always carry my seat with me.

"Okay, 'cept for my gall bladder."

"Gall bladder?"

"That's what my Jinshin therapist says. Gall bladder. Seems more like spleen to me."

"Spleen?"

He gave me a long look, mainly around my eyes. "Liver," he said.

"Liver?" This was getting ridiculous.

"Looks like you need your liver tweaked. Did you hear the news?"

"What's that?" I asked, relieved that he was willing to change the subject, whatever the subject had been. Liver?

"About Bill Evans. He got killed Sunday night."

"No shit? How?"

"He was beat up pretty bad. The cops aren't sure who did it, but they'll find out. He was a pretty weird guy, you know."

"No. I didn't know him much."

"Yeah. I used to ride with him when he still did some wranglin'. He was a little guy, but mean, you know?"

"A lot of little people are. Do you think he just got tanked up and got into a fight?"

"Yeah, well, that might have been it, but he was

into some other stuff, you know." Luke leaned to-ward me and dropped his voice. "He was selling shit on the side for a while, but then he found Jesus and got religious."

"What? Cocaine?" I asked. Maybe Luke knew something. Or he might just be bullshitting me to make himself look important.

But that was the end of it. Luke straightened up and smiled like a kid with a secret.

Two Game and Fish trucks pulled up and parked. They're called Division of Wildlife now, but the old name is locked in my brain, and it isn't impor-tant enough to make the effort to change. The war-dens got out and went into the doughnut shop next door.

"Hey, Luke, buy you some coffee?"

"Sure. That'd be great."

I bought two takeout cups, and we followed the game wardens into Geist's. There are plenty of chairs in the doughnut shop, but Geist's is another social center, and a lot of folks would rather stand around or lean on a saddle display than sit next door. It occupies the center of an invisible web of gossip, job possibilities, and messages for those of us with a loose set of mind and occupations to match. It's a stereotype of a mid-fifties TV western show backdrop. Luke fits right in. Maybe I do, too.

"Hey, Jim," I greeted Geist.

"Well, look who's up. And it's not even noon yet."

If Jim wasn't such a good friend, I'd take offense at the truth. He's short, stocky, and balding. He wears western boots, leather vests with conchas, and a bolo tie with a turquoise clasp. The outfit doesn't go too well with his horn-rimmed glasses, but he really is a sort of cowboy, just not the Marlboro variety. We go partners in the cattle business. He trucks them up to the ranch, helps with the branding and all in the spring and the roundup in the fall, and then trucks them back down to the Greeley livestock sale.

I nodded hello to the game wardens because we know each other by face if not by name, and the talk turned to hunting seasons and where the best herds of elk ought to be come fall. Jim always puts in for a draw license. I quit making useless donations to Game and Fish years back when the woods got too full of people and noise during archery elk season for me to have any luck. The stalk's the thing for me, not the kill, although I wouldn't pass up a winter's meat supply.

The younger of the wardens seemed edgy, but stayed quieter than usual. He kept looking questions at his senior, who kept not noticing. Finally he heaved an exasperated sigh.

"None of you guys interested in muleys?" he blurted.

The older guy raised his eyes to the ceiling. He watched us as we commented on our preference for elk over mule deer. It seemed to me he watched me closest.

"Remember the deadline for license applications is June sixth," he said after a lull. "If you're late we won't be able to draw our paychecks come July. Well, we'd better get to work. So long, Jim."

"See you later," he said.

"Take it easy," I added. They raised their hands in a general good-bye as they left the shop. There was silence while we watched them drive away, but after a few seconds of staring out his shop window, Jim spoke, without turning his head.

"Those guys are spending an awful lot of time around town these days. And they're not the only ones. They're up to something. I don't know what it is, but they're up to something."

I knew Jim, and his tone indicated that was the end of the subject.

I wandered over to look at a pair of boots. I'd need a new pair sometime before winter, and there's a ritual involved. I can't just walk in and buy a pair. No. I like to hint around at the purchase and let Jim see what he can scrounge up in the storeroom at bargain prices. Then I'll come in on rodeo day when he's busy as hell and the place is full of people. I don't really plan to do it, it's just that I'm in town anyway.

Jim watched me.

"Jim, Luke tells me we had a murder in town." I left it open-ended. Jim can be a better source of information even than Luke.

"That's right. It's in the papers, but there's not much there. I haven't heard anybody local talk about it yet."

"We certainly are getting to be big time," I said. "All the disadvantages of the big city right in our own backyard."

"Yep, big time," Jim agreed.

"Well, I have to take care of some things today. Sell me a can of saddle soap and a quart of neat's-foot oil, will you?" I said.

I paid up and thanked Jim, said good-bye to Luke, and left.

I didn't have anything definite to do, but the atmosphere at Geist's had had an odd feel to it. Luke had hardly said a word since we walked in. He'd stood off to one side watching the conversation. I wondered just what he knew about Bill's death and how I could get him to tell me. I went to my truck and took the dog for a walk before I had lunch at the Pines. I tried calling Sue again, but got no answer. When I was paying my check I asked the cashier when she was due in to work.

"She was supposed to work this morning, but she never showed. Why don't you ask over at the Holistic Health Center? She does massage out of there."

FOUR

I LOOKED UP the Holistic Health Center in the phone book and called to ask if Sue was there. A breathy female voice informed me she wasn't. I've met a lot of holistic health fanatics. There's no avoiding them around Cottonwood, but I could never figure why they all have the same spaced-out, quiet inflections. The only other group I know of that had that voice as a trademark were vegetarian peace and love devotees in the late sixties. Maybe it's a protein deficiency, or maybe they're the same people evolved with age, gone from youthful politics to middle-aged health concerns on their way to etheric retirement schemes.

I didn't feel like hanging around the Holistic Health Center on the off chance Sue might show up. I thought about what I'd learned from Luke. Motorcycles had come up twice now. And drugs and bikes run together a lot, at least in the rougher class of bikers. I filed the thought and stopped at the library to browse for an hour, but nothing caught my interest. I drove to the HHC.

The center is in a rambling old yellow house on the outskirts of town. The driveway crosses the creek on a wooden bridge that has just enough old-fashioned, old-timbered bounce to it so that, combined with the overhanging veil of cottonwood trees, crossing it seems to isolate you from the world. I drove across anyway.

I had to admit these folks had done a good job of cleaning up a Cottonwood eyesore. A little paint, carpentry, and some landscaping, and a good mood seemed to radiate from the place. I wasn't dead set against the holistic health movement. There's a lot of fraud and mumbo jumbo in it, and a lot of wishful thinking, but there's a diamond or two mixed with the coal. I've had a rubdown—pardon me, a massage—a time or two, and it can do wonders when a guy's tired and stiff or tense. Still, as with any movement where bucks and notoriety are possibilities, you get charlatans and charismatic leaders inventing jargon so their initiates can elevate themselves above the rest of us mortals.

What aggravated me as much as the mumbo jumbo just then was the parking lot. The spaces were lined out for midget Nipponese specials and the smaller chic Mercedes. Down at the end of the line, trying to be inconspicuous, were a '73 Buick, slowly rusting its life away, and a caved-in Chevy Nova. They were sporting bright-blue bumper stickers saying Visualize the Ozone.

"Neat trick, if you can do it," I muttered. I squeezed my Dodge pickup into two spaces next to a red Mercedes. Maybe it'd get lucky and some of my truck's class and style would rub off on it. Or maybe just some of the rust.

I got out and walked to the front door, noticing the Open sign in the window. When I tried the door it was locked, posted with a Back at 12:30 sign. It was about one. Business in the New Age. But then I don't watch the clock too closely myself.

The full lot meant there had to be people in the building, but I decided not to look for a second door. Sue's car wasn't in the lot, but it wasn't a tough walk from her house, and I knew her to be a willing conservationist. I went back and surveyed the rest of the parking lot for insightful statements on bumpers and windows. I Swam with Dolphins was next to a private flying club decal. This Car Protected by Good Karma. You Steal it, You Fix it. Touch Someone for Health. And a Screw Riceburners sticker on a BMW bike. I have a sticker or two on my truck: an airline employee parking tag from the previous owner that's outlasted the surrounding paint, and a county sticker that gets me into a landfill dump for free.

A man and a woman drove up in a Subaru wagon. They got out laughing. The man looked bigger than the car. He lumbered toward me like a freighter, smiling broadly, the woman a tiny skiff in his wake.

"Hi," he puffed. "Sorry we're late, but that's the way things go."

He put out his hand.

"Todd Stevens, director of Holistic Health Center. This is Serene Williams, our office manager."

"Hank Eston."

I shook his hand. Late thirties maybe, ruddy complexion, full beard, blond Prince Valiant haircut. He was wheezing, and there was booze on his breath. He looked like an overweight Viking out to conquer the business world in a used-car salesman's suit. Women would probably find him devastating except for the loose fat and sheer size of him.

Serene apparently did, from the way she kept her eyes on him. She was small, in her early twenties, brunette, light-boned, and softly pretty. She watched Stevens with the apprehension of a pup in training. Serene was not serene.

"What can we do for you?" Todd asked.

"I'm looking for Sue Fenton, and I thought she might be around here. She works here, doesn't she?" I asked.

"Susie? Oh yeah, sure. She's really a top-notch therapist, isn't she, Serene? Are you a client?"

"No, just a friend."

"Susie's not here right now, but come on in and let me show you around. We just got started here, you know."

"Serene," he said, turning to her, "would you finish those reports and get them ready for mailing? I'll drop them off at the post office later."

"Yes, Todd, right away."

Serene smiled at him, then briefly at me, and opened the office. Todd watched her backside as she walked ahead. When he saw me watching her he smiled. He laughed and started to put his arm around my shoulders, but I stiffened and he knew his mistake, removed his arm. I don't like hugging much, unless it's with the right sort of woman. A hug from a man is patronizing at best. For sure a man should never put his arm around a shorter man unless he wants to make an enemy, and for Todd Stevens that meant pretty much everyone

The office walls were business gray, decorated in the Popsicle colors of New Age art, with a liberal posting of licenses and professions of membership in different health organizations. Looking very much out of place, a Chamber of Commerce membership plaque stood atop a Kiwanis Club sticker on the desk. Serene was busy typing.

Todd caught me inspecting. "Pretty nice, huh?"

Most people I know stop fishing for compliments when they turn twenty-one.

"Very professional," I told him.

That brought a big smile. "Come on, I'll show you the whole place."

I had nothing better to do, so I followed him. We passed from the office into a lecture hall, then upstairs to a corridor lined with windows on one side and doorways opposite, each a different color.

"These are our treatment rooms," Todd said as he opened the first door, displaying a bright, quiet room containing desk and chair, a massage table, and two easy chairs.

"Pretty nice," I said. "How many people do you employ?"

"Oh, we don't employ the practitioners."

"You don't?"

"No. What we do at the Holistic Health Center is facilitate a networkage of efficacious combinations of independent specializings in the area of alternative health care practice."

"Huh?"

"We facilitate networkage," he explained, not at all. I dropped it and let him keep what was left of his smile.

An obscenely pink door opened and two women walked out talking. The younger of the two had to be the one working there. The other woman was dressed in a business suit, but the blonde was wearing a chartreuse T-shirt sporting the HHC logo and a pair of baggy, salmon-colored sweatpants.

"Hey, Junie," Todd called out as the two parted, "come on over and meet Hank. He's a friend of Susie's. This is Junie Flies-Like-an-Arrow Heglemeyer. She's a Rolfer."

"Hello-o-o," Junie crooned at me, sizing me up and down, but mostly middle. I wondered if my fly was open.

"Pleased to meet you, Junie," I said. "That's a pretty unusual middle name. Are you part Indian?"

"Junie's in the Women's Native Group," Todd said.

I didn't think I wanted to know what that might be, so instead I asked, "What exactly is a Rolfer?"

"Oh, we do deep tissue manipulation in order to remove bodily imbalance and realign the skeletal system."

"By deep tissue you mean muscle, not internal organs, I assume?"

She shook her head. "Not exactly—"

Todd jumped in. "What she means is, for instance, a misalignment of the vertebrae can lead to internal organ distress as well as back pain. An MD would prescribe pain pills. A chiropractor would do direct skeletal manipulation, but a Rolfer uses a special type of deep muscle massage to utilize the body's muscular strength to realign the spine. It really works."

"Interesting," I said.

"I also apply Chinese meridian and five-element theory," she added, "and read the Tarot." She paused and gave me the same sort of long look Luke had given me on the street. "Definitely kidneys."

"Kidneys?"

"Definitely."

I wanted to leave. It wasn't the technique so much as the people. I was about to tell Junie that it had been great and get the hell out when I was interrupted by a Buddha-bellied demon of good spirits whistling an Irish ditty. He was well into middle age, but above his two-day growth of beard he had the twinkling eyes of a leprechaun.

"Hey, ho! I'm Steve!" he bellowed. He gave Todd a hug, then turned to give one to me. I put my hand up, palm out, smiling. He shrugged and turned to Junie. "Hi, Flies-Like-an-Arrow. Give me a hug."

She did, enthusiastically.

"Are you here for one of my super-duper chakra balancings?" he asked me.

"No thanks. I'm just looking for Sue Fenton," I said.

He gave me one of those damned looks.

"Liver," he said.

"Sphincter," I said. I had to put a stop to this.

Todd interrupted. "Come on, Hank, let's go to the break room and you can meet some more of the people here."

There were five or six men and women in the room, all in their twenties, all talking at once, with mouths and both hands. When Todd walked in every one of them turned to look at him, smiling.

Todd said, "Hey, everybody, meet Hank Eston, a friend of Susie's."

I sidestepped an onslaught of hugging and nodded to them. Someone asked if I'd like something to drink, but I suspected it might be grape Kool-Aid, so I passed. Everyone but me looked as ecstatic as people at a religious revival meeting. Enough was enough.

"I guess I should be going. Thanks for the tour," I said.

"Sure. Stop by again. And here," he reached into a pocket and snapped a business card between his fingers, "come in for a free treatment sometime soon. You look like you need one." He paused awkwardly while I stared at him. "Everybody does.

"Well, kidneys," he mumbled, "or maybe liver. I'll tell Susie you were here."

I shook his hand, said thanks, and headed for the nearest exit.

When I fired up my truck the starter let me know it needed to be replaced. Again. The starter was an annual maintenance problem on my truck. I went straight home, where I keep a spare. There's nothing like a roll in the grease to end an unproductive day. I switched starters, cleaned up, and went inside. I looked at the sink, decided against cleaning house, and hit the refrigerator for a cold supper of salami, jalapeño peppers, and homemade sourdough bread. The holistic movement had me convinced. Only balanced meals from now on.

MAYBE THE BALANCED nutrition made a difference. I slept soundly and awoke Friday in a good mood, but I usually do when no one phones me out of my sleep. I let the Moose out and checked the sky, went in, and put some breakfast on the stove: coffee to boil, a pan full of thick bacon. I put my campstove toaster on a back burner with two slabs of home-made bread I'd sawed off the loaf.

I turned the bacon, buttered my toast, called in the dog, and started to eat my meal. The phone interrupted me.

I watched my breakfast grow cold as Sue told me she needed to work for a while, to make some money and settle her mind with routine. I told her I understood, and she invited me to lunch at her place next Tuesday.

I turned back to breakfast. While I ate I realized that no cops had wasted my time yesterday. The only thing different had been that I'd rummaged around Cottonwood instead of Pyrite Junction. Maybe I'd misinterpreted Riley's message. I tried to call for a copy of the coroner's report, but was told, "That report is not available to the public." Twice. I gave it up for the moment and decided not to press the pace.

I also decided that with the fences and loading chute and corrals all in good repair I could afford to take some time off to relax. But work is like any other drug when you're addicted. You can quit on any day, but it'll take five or ten days of concentrated effort at avoiding the stuff before you can forget about it and enjoy other things.

I tried. I gave it a hell of a try for half an hour,

then gave it up, convincing myself that doing little jobs around the place for myself would qualify as a break.

One comedy that plays every spring at eight thousand feet is guessing when to remove the snowplow frame from the truck. While I've seen it snow a foot and a half in mid-June, most springs don't demand road plowing after April. The snow melts off in a day or two, and a person ought to be patient enough to kick back and enjoy the cool before the summer heat sets in. I consulted my subconscious weather-forecasting department and decided to drop the plow frame.

Most snowplow frames are permanently mounted on a truck, but an old-timer taught me to mount a plow frame at the front of a truck and then about halfway back, behind the cab. I had one put together so the whole thing comes off by pulling four extra pins. The entire unit—blade, frames, cables, and all—goes on in twenty minutes and comes off in ten or so. I invested the ten minutes, dropped the plow behind the barn, and covered it with a tarp. The truck springs came up a couple of inches. Gas mileage would come up a mile or two per gallon. It was officially summer on the ranch, calendar be damned.

The dog and I chased each other for a few

minutes, until my addiction got the better of me again and I decided to set out the stock water tanks and get the piping hooked up from the spring that would keep them full by gravity flow. Five hundred-gallon stock tanks look huge, and a pickup truck only holds one at a time, but empty, one person can easily roll and push one wherever it needs to be rolled or pushed. It makes you feel like a circus performer rolling out the rings for a show. Pays about the same, too, but if money was the point I'd be wearing three-piece suits.

When that was done I got tools and work gloves from the barn and set out with the dog to make sure the few irrigation ditches on the place were clear and the headgates operational. Some summers are wet enough that the pasture rarely needs watering, but then some aren't.

Nothing had rusted up; all the gates raised and lowered easily. I greased the gearing and lopped the weeds growing on the banks, cleaning out the ditches where animals had broken them down.

It was a little early to bother pulling the bull thistle from the pasture. Later I wouldn't have to bend down so low. It's still easy enough to pull before it blossoms. Canadian thistle is another matter. I used a mattock to chop out any I saw. The experts claim that herbicides are the only way to control thistle. The road crews use it. One friend used to. The roads seem to have an awful lot of thistle. My friend has a tombstone. I find that a few days with a thick pair of gloves keep my fields pretty clean.

I walked, scything down golden banner before it bloomed and crowded the grass. I'd tried a gas-powered weed whacker. It saved perspiration, but cost me sore muscles and elbows. Plus the fumes and noise. I'd rather sweat, and weeding gives me a chance to see where the pocket gophers would require a little attention.

Technically the gophers are the property of Game and Fish, like any other wildlife. When you want to hunt them or use them in any way, the gophers are theirs. When they're digging up your pasture and leaving holes, Game and Fish figure they're yours.

I set up small windmill noisemakers to drive them onto someone else's property. It doesn't solve the problem in the large sense, but at least my conscience isn't offended by setting out poisoned grain.

The next morning I let the dog stay home. I was going to check for pine beetles and drop the infested trees in the sun to kill the insects.

Logging is hard, dangerous, dirty work, but you sleep well at night and you don't have to pay membership at a health spa. The noise and vibration of

a chain saw are annoying, but I'm not romantic
enough to use an ax and hand-saw on big trees.

I found, felled, and limbed the beetle trees before
heading home for a late lunch. I don't work long
in the woods, just hard. I got my day's work done
in about six hours and quit before I got sloppy.

FIVE

ON TUESDAY I spruced up and went to Cottonwood for my free lunch at Sue's. She met me at her door with a hug and a peck on the cheek.

"Sorry about getting you into all that trouble last week, but I didn't know who to call and you always said to call you if I needed anything and well..."

"That's all right, Sue. How are you doing now?"

"Okay, I guess, but come in, please. I'll get you a beer. Here, sit down at the table and I'll finish cooking lunch."

She brought me a bottle of Cooper's stout, remembering my taste after all the years. When I smiled my appreciation she patted my head and smiled, too.

"I told you I was sorry," she said.

Sue disappeared into the kitchen and I looked around her main room. The walls were hung with elaborately illuminated calligraphics, Chinese characters fitted into segmented concentric circles. I hadn't even noticed them last time I was there.

"What are these, Sue?"

"What?"

"These sketches on the wall."

"Oh. Horoscopes for my patients."

"Horoscopes. I've never seen any like these."

"They're based on the Chinese lunar calendar. They're a guide to the flow of *chi*, how the energy will flow in each client in each treatment. It's real complicated."

I looked again, but all I could make out were the names in English. I saw a chart for Todd Stevens and one still hanging there for Bill. I wondered if she'd predicted his death.

"Would you like one?" Sue asked. She came out of the kitchen, wiping her hands on a dish towel. "Give me the date, time, and location of your birth and I'll make one for you."

"Sue, you know I don't believe in horoscopes."

"Oh, come on, Hank. You can hang it in your cabin. It'll be beautiful and it'll be my way of saying thanks for being there last Monday. Please?"

"All right. 10 a.m. on January twenty-fourth, 1958, Clarksburg, West Virginia."

Sue wrote it down and returned to her cooking.

"I see you're still messing with herbs and things," I said, looking over her sizable collection of bottles and vials.

"Yeah. You ought to try some yourself sometime. They'd really be good for your liver."

Liver again. I sipped my stout. From the sounds of pots and knives in the kitchen, she was whipping up quite a feast.

All the labels were in Chinese. I picked up a vial. One bottle of green leaves looked and smelled like oregano. Probably was. Another held a gray powder. When I opened it and sniffed, I nearly gagged. It smelled like a tooth being drilled at the dentist's.

"Some of this stuff smells terrible, Sue."

"Yeah, but it works."

I put the bottle back and wandered over to inspect her de rigueur collection of rock crystals. Amethyst, of course, and some lapis. A piece of broken smoky quartz in matrix and a two-inch crystal ball. I tapped the ball with my fingernail to see if it was acrylic or real. Real.

Ah yes, I thought, the healing power of crystals. Devil's Head Mountain must be a terribly healthy place with all the crystals balancing out the gamma from the gadolinite. I ought to turn my rockhounding to a profit one day soon.

"Sit down. Lunch's ready."

I sat, expecting a truly great meal from all the preparation that had gone on.

"Here you are." She set a plate in front of me.

It was half full of brown rice, with a few small pieces of vegetables in sauce and a sliver of fish on top. A cute slice of orange on one side.

"My, my. Just look at that!" was all I could manage to say with any tact.

Sue beamed. I wondered what came after the appetizer, but then Sue sat down, too, and I knew. Nothing. I filled up on stout. Whatever became of women who know how much a working man eats?

After a few bites, I started hinting around about Bill's death, but Sue shook her head, swallowed hard, and looked at her plate, so I dropped it.

"How's work?" I asked. "Are you busy these days?"

"Oh yeah. In fact, I'm thinking of quitting the Pines soon. I have fifteen clients now, and I think I could easily find some more."

"That's great, Sue. It's got to beat waiting tables."

"It sure does."

We finished lunch and Sue announced that she had to go to work.

"Are you okay?" I asked. We hadn't talked much, but then comforting someone usually involves just being there. Running on at the mouth generally makes people wish you'd leave them alone.

Sue nodded her head.

"Stay in touch, Sue, will you?"

"Dear Hank." She gave me another kiss and hustled me out the door.

I went into town to try a call to Riley at the Sheriff's Department.

"Hello, Sergeant Riley. This is Hank Eston."

"Yeah, so what can I do for you?"

"Well, I've been nosing around a little and, well, I'm wondering what the coroner determined in Bill Evans's death."

"Are you now? So why ask me?"

"I figured you might be able to get me a copy of the report." I tried to sound optimistic, but I had my doubts.

"That investigation is still in progress, and even if it wasn't I wouldn't give you nothing. This isn't a public information service, you know. And a piece of advice for you. Keep out of this thing or you'll get yourself in even more trouble than you're already in."

I was confused for a moment, but then I figured he wasn't alone, or the recorder was on. I didn't say anything.

"Do you know if Bill was using any kind of shit? Heroin or cocaine?" he asked.

"No. Should I?"

"I got work to do. You just cool it."

"You mean that?" I asked. But he'd hung up on me.

I DECIDED TO FILL OUT my gourmet lunch with a burger at the Pines, but when I saw that Sue was working there and not at the Holistic Center as I'd assumed, it was either settle for dessert or insult her after all.

At least the company would be good. Brian Kells sat in the smoking section near a window, gray hair backlit, peering over his half glasses. Of my dozen or so regular customers for firewood, snowplowing, and general repairs, he is one of the few who is both cordial and interesting. I'd heard him describe himself as an orientalist, a consultant, and a teacher, but I couldn't see how he'd get anything for that in this area. He had a pleasant little house on thirty-five acres near the ranch. Small and trim, he looked like an academic in tweed and turtleneck, but I'd caught him a time or two at his house in a ratty old karate gi and he looked all right in that too.

"Hello, Eston," he greeted me. "And what has lured you from your sylvan sanctuary down to the temptations of the village?"

"I could ask you the same, you know. Good to see you."

I sat. Kells was the only person I'd ever known who called me by my last name and made it feel friendly. He was smoking and I accepted one of his Dunhills. He had a standard lecture on the idea that British cigarettes are harmless because of the standards set in the Pure Tobacco Act; it's the potassium nitrate and reconstituted garbage in American tobacco that do the damage. I didn't totally agree with him. Less harmful, maybe. I did agree with him that the whole anti-smoking campaign seems to combine with a lot of others meant to stamp out pleasure of any kind in a return to Puritanism. I figure you've got to enjoy what you can in life and pay the price when it's due. I borrowed Kells's matches and lit up.

"How many people have you talked to today?" he asked.

"Really only one. Why?"

"Here in town?"

"Yes."

"Was it liver, kidney, or gall bladder?" I thought about the stout Sue had given me. "Just liver today. Last time it came up it was two livers, one kidney, and a gall bladder, as I recall. You?"

"Kidneys, twice. Do you know why they always do that?"

I didn't know if I was being set up for a joke or a lecture. "No. Why?"

"Really first-class acupuncturists and other sorts of traditional Chinese and Japanese doctors look at skin color, the whites of the eyes, posture, all that, and can see which of the organic meridians need a needle or a poke or an herb," he told me. "So these New Agers give you a searching look and say 'gall bladder.' Makes them feel mysterious and competent."

"Which they aren't," I said.

"And it's charming just before lunch. Induces hypochondria, which is certainly good for their business. Not all like that, of course. Diane Meyer knows her stuff. Maybe one or two others."

"I've found everybody swears by holistic medicine until there's something serious. Then they're right down to the MD's."

"But everyone in this town is either a New Age Oriental Spiritualist Native American Crystal Massage Shaman, or the patient of one. Anywhere else in the world?"

"All of California, from what I hear."

Sue came to take our order, downcast and quiet. I didn't have the heart to order more than coffee after all. Kells seemed to catch something in my tone. He asked for a double order of carnitas and french fries, thinking I was broke and hungry, instead of just hungry.

"I don't like carnitas much, and I don't eat fries," he said when she'd left.

I thanked him and explained the situation. It seemed to amuse him.

"You heard about Bill Evans's murder?" I asked.

"Last week? Yes. You knew him?"

"Slightly. Sue happens to be—have been—his girlfriend. She's also an old flame of mine. She called me over the morning he died. I got there right in front of the sheriff."

"So you're the prime suspect? Triangle suspected? Jealousy the motive?" He looked up, not at me, but beyond. "Anything to it?" he asked.

"Jesus Christ! The Lord hateth a false witness. Not you, too?" I was mostly joking, but he didn't notice. China clattered just behind my ear. I turned.

"Sorry."

Sue stood stock still, tray in one hand, the other raised in front of her in something between a fist and a claw. It took her several seconds to slack it off. When she put the coffee cups on the table it was slow as *t'ai chi ch'uan*. Her eyes were glazed, watching heaven.

"I'll have your food in a minute," she said to Kells in an odd, dreamy voice.

"Take your time," he said softly, in a tone much like hers.

Sue must have backed away very slowly, from the way Kells stayed still. I knew she was gone when he let out a deep breath and shivered.

What touched that off? What the hell had happened?

"What does she do other than wait tables?" he asked.

"Massage. At the Holistic Health Center and at home."

"A Chinese system," he said.

"I suppose. Swedish is out of fashion, isn't it?"

We drank our coffee. Kells was thinking hard, or listening to some inner voice. I was full of questions, but couldn't frame the first one. After a while he looked at me. His eyes were sad.

"Can I help you with this?" he asked.

"I don't see how, I can't really do anything with it. I don't have much to go on. Bill may have been dealing something, but I don't know much about the drug scene. I was hoping to get a look at the coroner's report, but caught a load of crap when I asked for it."

"Hmm. Perhaps I can help you there. One of my

calligraphy students is an assistant DA. Takayama.''

"I think I saw him when I was in for questioning.
You teach Japanese writing to a Japanese?''

"He's nisei. They spoke it some at home when
he was a child, but he never learned to read or write
it. Not unusual for the Japanese. Chinese tend to
keep their culture whole when they emigrate. The
Japanese-Americans dump it and only take it up
again as a hobby when they're older.''

Sue brought the food, all brisk and back to
"Anything else? More coffee?'' Kells arranged his
dishes for my discreet access. We ate. It helped. He
picked up the check. I nodded my thanks as we
walked outside.

"You'll call me if you get anything on that report?''

"Sure. A day or two, I expect.''

"Thanks.''

"Hank,'' he said, stopping, looking squarely at
me, "be damned careful.''

I told him I would. He waved and crossed the
street to his car, a battered old Subaru wagon that
ill-suited him. I wondered what had caused the
warning and what the hell had happened there in
the Pines. I didn't much care for the connections I
seemed to be making.

SIX

I GOT A CALL that night for an emergency—read big-bucks—job to do the next day. Someone's well wasn't pumping. I accepted because that's how I earn what little I do. It's why I put up with a phone. So Wednesday morning I left Musashi at home and drove to town to check the job and put together a materials list.

The Harrisons had gotten my name from the local hardware store. When I arrived at their house I forgot about the big bucks. It was a small, neat little place that showed the signs of being maintained with all the resources that pride, elbow grease, and an empty bank account could provide. Harrison opened the door and stood with an arm around his wife's waist. A couple of gray-haired teenagers still madly in love with each other.

"Come in, please. Thank you for coming so soon. I know you must be busy," he said.

"Well, it's kind of important to have your water working, right?"

They both straightened their backs a little. He looked me hard in the eyes and said, "We lived here for fifteen years without a well. Hauled all our water from the town pump. We'll do it again if need be. The well's just convenient, that's all."

His wife relaxed and slapped his arm gently. "Hush, you." She smiled at me and added, "It's true, you know. We did. But now we're not set up for that anymore, and we need that well fixed no matter what it costs."

"If the danged thing's gone dry, we're not going to drill a new one at our age," Harrison put in, and then said cautiously, "How much do you charge, anyway?"

I thought a few seconds. If I charged too much their finances would keep them from getting things fixed. If I charged too little, their pride would do the same.

"For something like this, if I can fix it, how does eight dollars an hour sound? No charge if I don't fix it," I added.

"That sounds fair, doesn't it, Dale?" Mrs. Harrison asked.

"It sounds fine," he said, but his face indicated he had a little discomfort with it. Maybe I should have said six. Some elderly folks don't keep track of current prices.

"Come on in, son. We can't offer you coffee, with no water, but how about a can of pop?" he asked.

"That'd be great." I watched him go to the kitchen and open the refrigerator. The empty spaces told me I'd guessed right about their income. I wasn't going to make much money, but I'd feel pretty good.

"Root beer okay?" he asked as he handed me a can.

"My favorite, as a matter of fact. Thanks." I took a few sips. "Where are the well pump controls?"

"Downstairs. Follow me."

I checked the feed wires for juice and tried the reset button. No go. The pressure gauge was at zero, so I pulled the cap on the pressure switch. The contacts were open when they should have been closed. I pushed them together and the pump kicked in.

"Is that all it was? Shoot, I could have done that myself," he said.

I let go of the switch and it opened again. "You need a new pressure switch."

"How much will that cost me?"

"Probably ten bucks and maybe an hour of my time. Okay?"

"Okay. Go and get her."

I pushed the contacts shut to fill the pressure tank and said, "That'll give you about forty gallons to use till I get back. I'll be as quick as I can."

"We'll be waiting for you."

I went to town for the switch. On the way back from the hardware store I passed the Holistic Health Center and saw Sue's car parked in the lot. I thought I'd see how she was, so I turned around and pulled in.

In the office, Todd and Serene were talking to a middle-aged, serious-faced man in cowboy boots and Levis. A check was lying on the desk.

"Hi, folks," I said when the conversation paused. "I saw Sue's car and thought I might talk to her."

The stranger was staring at me. Not wanting to be impolite, I returned the favor and introduced myself.

Stevens said, "This is Amos Johns, one of Sue's clients."

"Pleased to meet you," I said, and we shook hands, still studying each other.

He wasn't a very big man, but he looked wiry and tough. The scuff marks on the sides and insteps of his boots told me he spent a lot of time in a saddle. Scars and calluses on his hands, and the crow's-feet at his eyes, said he was a ranch hand,

too. Then I saw something that made me postpone
the Harrisons' plumbing repair. He was wearing a
crucifix, odd enough among holistic clients in Cottonwood. But what caught me was that it was an
unusual one, hammered silver with arms half the
span of the standard pattern, and it matched the one
I'd seen on Bill Evans's body. I looked back up to
his eyes.

"You know, I'd sure like to talk to you sometime," I said.

"No time like the present," he said, "but I'm a
busy man. Idle hands, you know. You're welcome
to come out to my place if you want, and we can
talk while I do some chores."

"Sounds good to me." I wasn't going to miss
the chance. I turned to Stevens. "Tell Sue I was
by, will you? Thanks." I left, dodging good-byes,
and waited in my truck for Amos Johns to come
out.

"Follow me," he said. I was pleased to see him
head for a pickup that resembled mine in its state
of decay. It would be a place to begin.

AMOS JOHNS LIVED a pretty good ways out of town,
up Buffalo Park Road on a working ranch of high
meadow surrounded by wooded hills. The barns
and corrals were in good shape, so he wasn't too

broke, but they weren't up to polo club standards. There were just enough horses to work the cows he was running. A practical man. We'd get along fine.

We pulled up near the barn and parked. I asked if I could use a phone to call the Harrisons and beg a little time from them. Johns led the way into his tack room. I made the call and walked outside.

He came out with a toolbox, chaps, and a twitch. He didn't say anything or even look my way, just headed for a corral holding two horses and, I noticed, an anvil mounted on a stump. I followed him. He held the gate open for me and I latched it behind. We walked to the anvil. He set the box down, put on his chaps, and grabbed a halter and lead rope hanging on a post, holding the twitch out, blind, in the other hand to me. I took it. First chore looked to be shoeing horses, and I was there. That made me free help, but I didn't mind. I'm a practical man, too.

"We'll do the bay first," he said and pointed at the twitch. "You probably won't need that for him, but keep it handy."

I nodded, and he went to put the halter on the horse. He came back and held the lead out to me, just like the twitch, without looking, taking for granted my hand would be there and that I'd know what to do with it. He must've figured that anyone who drives an old pickup and wears scuffed boots would share his knowledge of everything. I took the rope. Johns went to the toolbox and came back with hammer and nippers, a rasp, and a couple of cold shoes, which he tossed by the anvil. He came to me and the horse, looked at how I was holding the lead, then turned his back to me, bent down, took a front hoof, and started cleaning it.

"How do you know Sue Fenton?" he asked me.

"She was a girlfriend a while back. Now just a friend."

"That so?" A long pause. "What makes you want to talk to me?"

I decided to be blunt, my best, natural style.

"You're wearing a cross and that's something you don't see very often at the Holistic Health Center. Also, it's the same kind Bill was wearing the last time I saw him."

"Billy Evans. Sue's live-in."

I didn't miss the disapproving inflection.

"Yeah."

"When's the last time you saw him?"

"A week ago Monday, when the coroner was covering him up."

"The hell you say."

"Sue called me over for help that morning."

"Hmmph." Another pause. He cut the clinches

off the nails and pulled the old shoe. "Gimme that rasp."

"The sheriff thinks I'm involved in that. I'm not. I'm trying to find out who is so I can get myself cleared."

He finished filing the hoof and began to shape a new shoe on the anvil. I waited a little, then added, "Bill didn't strike me as the kind of guy who'd be wearing a crucifix."

Amos Johns looked up at me. "And just what kind of guy would be wearing a crucifix? Tell me that."

"Well, he just struck me as a sort of lowlife. A motorcycle jacket and a Maltese cross, maybe, but not a crucifix."

Amos Johns kept staring at me. "Judgmental, aren't you?"

He was reminding me of someone I used to know in Cottonwood. A half-crazed construction worker turned part-time...

"You ever hear the story of Paul on the road to Damascus?" he asked.

...preacher. "What church do you belong to?" I asked.

"Bright boy. I'm pastor of the Redemption Church in Kittredge. You ought to come by some Sunday. You need it."

"What makes you think so?"

He beat the horseshoe again, then paused, looking past the anvil at the hills.

"Everybody does." He turned to face me and added, "Billy did, by gosh! It turned his life around."

He came back to put the shoe on. He was right. It had turned Bill's life around as far as it could go.

"How did Bill end up coming to your church, if I can ask?"

"I hired him for help putting in some fences, and we talked. A lot about him and what he was doing with his life. We talked about me and what I was doing with mine. I guess he thought I was getting a better deal, and hell, he just broke out crying the third afternoon, right out there, by that stretch post. The Holy Spirit just fell on him and slayed him down to the ground."

"What do you mean, 'slayed him down'? Did he have a heart attack?" I asked. I got another hard, gray-eyed glance.

"Don't interrupt me. We spent the rest of the day talking, reading the Book together. I invited him to join our fellowship and he did. Started coming three or four times a week."

"How long ago was this?" I asked.

"Three, no, four weeks ago. Bill didn't have long

in this world, but maybe the Good Lord figured he'd learned what he needed to know and it was time to call him home to his reward.''

''It looked to me more like someone sent him home,'' I said. I was thinking of the bruises I'd seen and the fact that Bill Evans was only thirty-one.

Amos Johns stopped work and straightened up, staring into my eyes. I always wonder what people see when they stare at me. I judge other people by their eyes, too, but I've been wrong enough times to know you don't always see the whole truth.

''I'm fifty-three years old,'' he said, ''and I've seen a lot.'' He held up his hands, knuckles out. ''I drank hard, rode hard, fought hard, loved hard. I still do. Man's not perfect, but we're God's creation and we're made the way we are. We do the best we can, as each of us sees fit. None of us is better than the other. Bill's best just wasn't too good some of the time, that's all.''

He was staring at me still, and I got the impression he'd said all he was going to say about Bill, when his eyes slid past me and focused on something in the distance behind me. I turned to look.

''Damn 'em,'' he cursed. ''There's a few of Bill's old friends now. See 'em? Over on that west hillside. Three guys.''

I looked left and scanned the hill about half a

mile away. Halfway up, maybe two hundred feet above the meadow, I saw three men carrying something black and heading obliquely up the hill.

"Yeah, I see them. Who are they?"

"Come on. I might need a hand."

He took the lead from me and removed the halter from the bay, tossed both over a rail, and put his tools together, outside the corral.

"They're my neighbors, if that's the word for them. Poaching again. I've told them plenty of times to stay off my place."

"Why don't you call the sheriff?" I asked.

"Sheriff, hell. You ever meet one that's going to walk up that hill? Or get here before they're gone?" He pointed to the hillside and sprinted for his truck. "Come on."

I went. We bounded across his meadow at about sixty miles per hour, but I give him credit. He knew how to do it, just where every bump and ditch was hidden, and he missed them all. But then he said he rode hard. I found out he also walked hard. We caught up with his neighbors pretty quick, but maybe the fact that they felt like talking to him had something to do with that. I was slightly winded from the climb, but Amos Johns had his back up and that helped him a bit.

"What the hell do you three think you're doing here?" he yelled at the center man.

"What's it look like, Pop?"

His two friends were sizing me up. They were all in dirty jeans and motorcycle boots. The middle one was clean-shaven, wearing one of those leather Brando caps. We were about six feet apart, Amos on my left. One of them made a move to circle to my right, to get behind me, but I set my left foot back a step and put my arms across my chest, forearms unlocked, shaking my head just a hair, raising one eyebrow. He stopped, licked his lips, and made a mean little smile. The third guy dropped the black trash bag he was holding, and it settled with a rattle. That was it.

Amos said "Shit." Softly.

I had time to say, "I'm with you," and we were on.

It wasn't my fight, but I was in it. Three against two isn't exactly even, and three young guys against a fifty-year-old offends my sense of fair play, though Amos was a pretty tough fifty-year-old. And we were still on his property Also, I had no choice. It may take two to tango, but you don't have to fight to get your head beat in.

I saw the center, clean-faced guy and the black-bearded man on the left move into Amos out of the corner of my eye, but Smiley in front of me was closing the distance. I let him come on. Johns would have to hold his own until I got free of my immediate problem.

Smiley feinted left and then tried to kick me in the crotch with his right foot. Stupid move. I crouched down a little and grabbed his pants leg, then pushed up and out. I put my weight on my left leg and buckled his left knee with my other foot. He went down hard on his back and neck. I kicked him once in the ribs, but he didn't respond. I knew he'd stay down. If something's important enough to fight about, fight.

Amos Johns was still standing, but I didn't know how. One bastard had his back to me, holding him while his buddy did the punching. I had heavy boots on so I didn't want to kick him in the spine. Too much effort to lift a size twelve that high. I snapped the outside edge of my hand into the side of his neck and now the odds were reversed. The third guy got in one last punch to Amos Johns's stomach, but I pushed in from the side and let myself be the target.

This guy was a lot better than his partners. He got me once each in the face and the chest before I put a solid one straight out, into his sternum. It slowed him up enough to let me put another one a

little lower and off to the side. I made sure his floating ribs were riding high tide, and that was enough
for him. He took off as fast as his pain would let
him.

I looked to make sure the other two were still
out of action, then helped Amos to his feet. I was
okay, just some minor cuts and bruises, but Amos
looked the worse for wear.

"You okay?" I asked.

"Yeah, I'm okay," he said, but he winced when
he took a step and picked up the bag his neighbors
had been carrying.

"What's wrong?"

"My back, damn it."

"Need a hand?" I moved toward him.

"No. Let's get back to the truck."

He took another step and stopped, held his arm
up and out to the side for help. He shook his head
to curse his injury, but said nothing. I got under his
arm to hold him up and we walked back. By the
time we made the truck he was shaking, and it was
a warm day.

"You'd better drive," he said, and threw the bag
in the bed of the truck.

I nodded and helped him in. I drove back to his
barn as fast as I could go safely and helped him out
when we got there. He was in bad shape.

"Just let me sit down inside."

"I'd better call an ambulance for you. You don't look too good."

He was pale and I could see he was still shaking. I didn't figure it was just excess adrenalin burning off after the fight.

"No, I'll be all right. Just wait awhile."

He didn't move inside, but slid to the ground, his back riding the barn wall down. A couple of minutes passed and he looked up at me, half apology and half worry.

"Maybe you'd better make that call after all. In the tack room."

I ran for it and called an ambulance.

"Your address?"

"I don't know it. Can't you use the 911 system?"

"You're on a party line. It won't identify the location. I need a street number."

That again. "Look, I don't know it. Let me give you directions."

I did.

"Your name?"

"Just get here fast. The man's name is Amos Johns. He's at the barn."

"We have to have your…"

I hung up and ran back outside, grabbing some

saddle blankets on the way. Amos Johns was lying on the ground when I reached him, but he was still conscious and alert. I laid a blanket on the ground.

"Can you roll onto this?"

"Yeah, I think so. Thanks."

I covered him with two more and told him how things stood.

"I can't stay here. The sheriff already suspects me in Bill's death and I'd be in deep trouble showing up at another beating. You see how it is."

"I see it," he said. He'd stopped shaking. "One thing before you go. Take that bag with you, will you? So they can't come back for it."

I pulled it out of his truck and went back to him.

"Are you going to be okay until the ambulance gets here? Maybe fifteen minutes or so? If you aren't sure, I'll stay, but it'd be best for me to get the hell out of here."

"I'll be fine, son. And I won't say a word about who you are. Count on that."

"Sure you're okay?"

"Fine. Now get gone."

I ran for my truck, tossed the bag in the bed, and jumped into the cab. I felt like an ass, putting myself out of trouble by leaving, but I really couldn't do anything for him by staying.

"Show up in church sometime," he called out.

"I'll do that, for you," I yelled as I backed the truck around and tore out of there.

I made it to a side road without being seen. I went back to town and finished the Harrisons' repair job, then headed straight home.

I threw a pack together, put the horses out to pasture, and hustled the dog into the truck. I was about to head out when I remembered the plastic bag in the truck bed. I pulled it out and walked over to the manure pile, still a good six feet high at the center. I tossed the bag to the very top. It clattered when it landed. I was torn for a moment between curiosity as to what was in it and the urge to get the hell out. Well, that manure pile wasn't half as inviting as fishing in the high country. I wanted to think and I didn't want any unnecessary intrusions during the process. I left.

SEVEN

ABYSS LAKE IS close by air but hard to get to on the ground, and the trout are usually good there. The weather was clear and bright, still early and cool enough at that altitude so mosquitos were only a minor nuisance. Gravel and soft grass alternated underfoot, blending crunch and squish into a kind of music. There were patches of brush and reeds, but the trees left the lake a lot of room. I planned to fish and think and relax, if I could.

I threw a lot of casts and did a lot of thinking, but got no results. Amos Johns had said his neighbors were old friends of Bill's, and said it in a way that implied they were not exactly pillars of society. He also said they were poachers. Maybe Bill had been a poacher too. There should be lots of elk around Amos Johns's place, deer, too, from the looks of it, but Sue didn't eat meat, wouldn't allow it in the house. If Bill had found religion he would have wanted to go a hundred percent straight for a while, until he realized that he couldn't eat what the sparrows and the lilies of the field eat, even if that was all Sue was willing to feed him.

So what were they doing with the meat? Selling it? Restaurants that offer wild game wouldn't buy it, would they? They'd need records of purchase, and it'd be a hell of a lot easier to buy it legally from a ranch that raised it. And not much more expensive, either, I bet. An individual might buy it, but why not shoot it themselves and save money if they wanted to risk a jail term anyway? Fewer accomplices that way.

If Bill had gotten religion like Amos Johns said and had quit poaching, would that be enough cause for his cohorts to beat him to death? Not likely. And the cops were hinting around about drugs. There'd be enough money in that to kill someone, but not in elk meat.

I spent two days gnawing around the edges of it and gave it up. I stuck to fishing and rockhounding, although I couldn't completely clear my mind.

On Sunday afternoon, a game warden came out of nowhere to check my license, the older of the two who'd been at Geist's. They must use satellite surveillance or some sort of psychic radar to find people. He came up from the wrong side of the divide to have seen my truck, and not many people are going to hike ten miles up to fish. It's one of life's mysteries.

"This dog's supposed to be on a leash," he said, greeting me.

The dog was running mad circles around him, jumping in the air and trying to get him to play.

"Does he chase game?" he asked.

"In three years of life, he's managed to pin a few rabbits and bumped into two porcupines and lost, but he's never injured anything and he doesn't chase big game," I said.

"Well, given that he's such a vicious animal and that this is such a populous area," he grinned, rubbing Musashi's ears, "I suppose I could let it slide. If you have a fishing license on you."

"I sure do."

I showed it to him. He looked at the holster on my hip and I looked at his. For both of us the guns were just tools to be used when necessary. I carry the extra three pounds around backpacking in case I run into two of the four common dangers in the Rockies, feral dogs and violent men. It doesn't help with the other two, dysentery and ticks. He gave back my license and I put my wallet away.

"Can I offer you a cold pop?" I asked. I pulled a five-can six-pack out of the lake.

"Well, thank you, you certainly can."

He sat and popped the top. The dog sat next to him, glad to have a new face, or rather smell, around.

"But it'll cost you," I said, smiling as I opened one myself.

He put on a mock serious face. "Then I guess you'd better show me a sales tax license for this, your place of business," he said, rolling his eyes around the woods.

I laughed. "First, how the hell do you guys show up in the middle of nowhere to check someone's license?"

"That, my friend, is one of the mysteries of the guild, and we're sworn to professional secrecy."

Then I had an idea about Bill's death. "Not that I'm planning to go into the business, but what does elk meat, say, out of season, sell for?"

He turned very earnest. "Why do you ask?"

I studied his face a moment, sized him up as a straight shooter, and decided to lay it out. I told him about Bill's death and the suspicion sitting on me, and I told him I had a hunch that Bill had been involved in a poaching ring.

"There's not that much money in it," he said. "These days, around here it'd be easier to make a living working at a regular job."

"And the guy had a regular job."

"Well, you never know about someone. Maybe he wasn't too bright. You have any names for me?" he asked. "There's a reward for information on poaching."

I considered telling him about the incident at Amos Johns's ranch, but then remembered I wasn't tied to that yet and I'd be opening myself up for more trouble. I shook my head.

"Not yet. I would guess the sheriff has an idea by now."

"The sheriff," he growled. "You know who's got the case?"

"A Sergeant Riley, I think. At least that's who interviewed me."

"Riley. He thinks his work stops where the pavement ends."

I didn't comment. He seemed to have something more to say.

It took him a while, sipping his drink, looking out over the snowcaps and the blue beyond. Then he shifted on his haunches and pulled out a pack of cigarettes and lit up.

"We haven't seen any evidence of anyone poaching elk," he said. "You sure it's elk?"

"No."

"We're finding some strange remains out here lately. Weird."

"What?"

"Muleys."

He got up, stuck the smoke in his mouth, crushed the pop can, flipped it from hand to hand a few times, and then deposited it in the plastic bag I'd set out for trash. Then he took a long drag and put the cigarette out under his heel.

"Muleys, shot with an ought-six and mutilated."

I gave him twenty seconds. He didn't even blink.

"Mutilated how?" I asked quietly.

"Antlers hacked off with a bow saw, I'd say. Dicks cut off with a knife."

"What the hell for?"

"That's what we'd like to know. And who. Most of all, who those sick bastards are."

"I guess it might be the same guys. Maybe get some names from Riley, if he's got anywhere."

"Riley. Shit."

"Well, someone in the department, maybe."

"Yeah. Well, thanks for the drink." He stretched.

I called my dog.

The warden walked toward the trees, turned, and raised his hand in farewell, then headed off to find another fisherman who thought he was isolated in the wilderness experience. I threw my line out in the water and tried to relax. But I didn't, of course.

I reeled in my line and tried another cast, but the trout weren't interested in what I was offering. The Moose was looking at me, wondering when I'd stop my nonsense and do something worthwhile, like throw a stick or go for a walk.

"Maybe you're right, big fella. This sure isn't working." Talking to one of your fellow animals may seem strange to someone who's never spent much time alone with one. Most people keep their mouths going constantly with their own species, whereas, if they'd experiment, they'd find that a dog or a horse can fill the same need as a human being: letting you run on at the mouth and walking away after a reasonable amount of time. Except nonhumans usually pay more attention to what you say. Conversation is mostly a social interaction anyway, not an exchange of information, and personally, I find that my dog makes for better society than most humans I've met.

Moose was running in mad circles in his excitement. I reeled in again and put my rod next to my pack. I took my rock hammer and Moose and I went for a walk.

As I said before, a walk can be a great stimulant to mental maneuvers. Especially a walk through the back country. There's something about long vistas of high peaks that makes a person get a large perspective of whatever problem he's working on. The cold freshness of the air keeps you alert even under the hot midday sun.

My feet picked their own path and I let my thoughts do the same.

So. It looked like Bill was in with the poachers, got religion, got disgusted, and wanted out, and they beat him up to discourage him from leaving or talking. They discouraged him all right. Permanently.

I knew three of them by sight, and so did Amos. Amos might even have a name or two. If that plastic bag on my manure pile had in it what I thought it did, we'd be pretty close to sewing them up on the poaching thing, if not the murder.

But what the hell were they taking antlers and penises for? Satanic rituals? Some weird old Arapaho hallucinogen or the latest designer drug? Or was the mutilation of the deer a sick ritual in itself, and the antlers and dicks only trophies?

There was one other thing bothering me. Three bruises on the back and a few cuts on the face just hadn't looked like enough to kill Bill Evans.

I've developed a system over the years. Let it all stew in your brain long enough and at some point your gut and your brain come into agreement. Your whole being tells you when you're right. Most of the time. If your head's screwed on properly and if you're in tune with your life and your environment.

My friend Kells, steeped in his Zen mystique, would say that you need to fight the battle within, calm yourself, and gain harmony with your demons, and then the battle with the external enemy is won. I say a rose by any other name will still prick your hand if you grab it too fast and too hard. It comes to pretty much the same thing in the end, I guess.

Kells would probably have the autopsy report from Takayama when I got back. It might answer a question or two.

So Moose and I walked, and I let my brain and body work together to come up with a plan. We played a little fetch-the-stick and I broke open a few rocks, looking for that perfect topaz crystal I wanted to send to my niece for Christmas.

We wandered back to camp in time for sundown and dinner. I tried a few casts and hot damn! The fish were biting. No canned stew tonight. Fresh fish, fried in butter. Things were looking up.

I sat by my dinner fire, drinking coffee and smoking a few cigarettes, thinking. The problem was how to get the information to Riley and not get myself into a worse jam doing it. I figured I could go to see Amos, lay it out for him, and get him to take it to Riley.

Once, I had packed out of similar country at night with no moon, and it took me all night to cover six miles. It's hard not to go into action immediately once you finally get a plan, but then sometimes it keeps you from breaking your legs. I would stay the night and walk out next morning.

Besides, the sky is pitch black that high up, and with no city lights to wipe out half the constellations, the night sky is a show to be enjoyed at every opportunity. I got into my sleeping bag and watched the stars wheel.

There was still something wrong with it. It was like an animal standing stock still in the timber, because he knows you're there. There's only one way to find him. Scrutinize each little piece of the picture head on and it'll take you forever. Keep your eyes open and scan the woods for the pattern that doesn't fit the trees and it will flash out at you from the side of your vision. Of course, astigmatism helps. You see things a little differently than most people.

So I let It go and drifted away from the stars into sleep. I was fumbling open a black plastic bag, feeling sad and a sense of foreboding. The plastic was difficult and my hands weren't working well. Finally It came open. Deer antlers. Bloody deer antlers in the velvet. Too much blood for antlers. Soft stuff in the bottom. I didn't want to reach down into the soft stuff. I felt the soft stuff through the plastic. Tubular lengths, sausages. Not sausages. Penises in blood soup. One of them was mine.

I woke to find Musashi's nose in my ear, the sky still coated with starlight.

"It's okay, boy, it's okay," I told him.

But it wasn't really. It wasn't going to be as simple as sending Amos to Riley.

EIGHT

As SOON AS I got back to the ranch I gave Amos Johns a call, but got no answer. I called patient information at several Denver hospitals until I located him at Saint Olaf's. I showered and changed clothes and drove down to visit him. He must have been hurt worse than I thought.

"Hank Eston, as I live and breathe. How are you, son?" he asked, reaching to shake my hand.

"I'm not the one in the hospital bed," I said. "How are you? They told me you were still in guarded condition downstairs."

"What do they know? I'm fit and ready to go." He thumped his chest and winced. "Well, ready to go, anyway. The doc was just here and gave me the okay. The people downstairs haven't got the word yet, but it's not surprising. This has got to be the worst-run place I ever saw. Everything smells like boiled chicken grease and looks worse. They got something mixed up with my IVs the first day

I was here and sent me into delirium. I dang near died before one of the interns bothered to actually read my chart and caught it. Anyway, they had their chance. They couldn't kill me in five days so they'll have to let me go home. I guess tomorrow."

"What did they find wrong?" I asked.

"I got one kidney all beat to hell and a lot of bumps and bruises. The facial stuff will only make me more handsome. I thought you were watching my back," he said.

"I did as quick as I could, but I had to take care of the third guy first. Sorry."

"Don't give it a second thought. I'm going to be fine. Come to think of it though, I don't remember ever getting hit from the back. There was just that one guy holding me."

"I'm afraid I was a little too busy to notice."

I picked up my hat. It's a rule of mine to keep hospital visits short and bright. It didn't seem quite time to tell him the tale or ask him for help.

"Come see me at the ranch sometime after tomorrow," he said.

"For sure."

I said good-bye and headed out of Denver on Sixth Avenue, then I-70 to go through Cottonwood and use my bank's ATM machine to draw a little cash from my account. I stopped and did it, wrangled the truck through the light on Main Street, and headed home.

I was halfway to Pyrite Junction on 73, going through the curves where the hillside comes down nearly sheer on the left and the right shoulder drops off ten feet into the creek bed, when a black, chopped-down Harley with the customary bad mufflers came up behind me. There was a passing zone coming up and he could get by me soon. I looked back to the road ahead. No oncoming traffic. I heard the bike accelerate to pass. He stayed alongside me too long. I looked left to see why and got a head-on view of a sawed-off shotgun barrel.

I dove to the right, flat as I could get on the seat. I couldn't hit the brake in that position, but my foot came off the gas when I started to move and slowed the truck enough to put the blast into my fender more than my door. The Harley took off. I straightened up in time to stay out of the creek, took several deep breaths to calm down, then drove like hell to the pay phone in Pyrite Junction. I hadn't seen much of the rider's face—the shotgun barrel had sort of occupied my attention—but I was sure it had to have been one of the poachers from the fight on Amos's hill. I thought it was the big one with the black beard.

I took my .38 Special from the pocket in the seat

cover and kept it with me while I called for a deputy to meet me. I like to keep it handy whenever I can. I watched everyone who drove by, walked by, or showed themselves in any door within five hundred yards. I was shaking a little, now that it was over, with excess adrenalin. I keep hearing about people who stay completely calm both during and after something like that, but I have to settle for during.

When the Sheriff's Department arrived, one man, one hour later, he examined my truck and asked for my account of what happened. I told him.

"Did you get a license number?"

"You've got to be kidding."

"We can't do much without a license number. Can't stop every loud motorcycle going down the road."

"The bastard tried to kill me!"

"Watch your mouth. As far as I can tell it looks like you got hail damage to your truck."

"On one side? On a vertical surface?"

"Yeah. Hail damage. Maybe from heavy winds. Dispatch told me when I got this call to be careful, you might try to give a false report. Like for insurance purposes or something."

"I don't carry comprehensive on this old beast.

Why in hell would I do that? That's a shotgun blast. Anyone can see that.''

"I can't. Too bad about your insurance. You ought to switch your policy. So long." And he left.

So much for serving and protecting. I could go home and forget about an attempt on my life. I could go home and cower helplessly, as many crime victims do.

No, I couldn't.

This was the third time I'd come across the subject of motorcycles, and this time it wasn't just conversational. I drove back to Cottonwood.

I parked the truck in the lot near the creek, stuck the .38 under my shirt, and walked down Main Street to the Buck. It's illegal to carry a gun concealed, but I figured this was a time when it was better to get caught with it than caught without it.

The Buck is a run-down bar that attracts people from all over Denver on weekends, when it uses some country rock and heavy-metal stars as a draw. If the lighting wasn't so bad and the building painted brown inside and out, it'd be closed down as a health hazard. I checked the line of bikes parked out front. Most of them were too clean to belong to the people I wanted to talk to, but one or two looked promising. I went in.

I stood just inside the door until my nose got

accustomed to the stench and my eyes to the dark.
Then something I didn't want to happen happened.

"Hey, Hank Eston! Over here."

Luke Sigilli was standing at the bar. There wasn't
any choice but to join him. I ordered a bottle of
Miller, and another Bud for Luke. Since the place
started getting so wild they quit serving in glass
mugs. I refuse to drink out of a plastic cup.

I leaned into Luke, no easy job, with him smell-
ing like rotting Mexican food. "Quietly," I said.

"Why?"

"A little over an hour ago I got shot at out on
seventy-three. The guy who fired might be in here.
Biker, big, black beard. Seen anyone like that?"

"Someone like that was here for a half hour or
so, about ten minutes ago. Noisy damn bike. He sat
with those two over there by the stage."

I turned around and leaned my back against the
wood, surveying the room. The two most likely
owners of the hogs outside were sitting together at
a table near the stage. One of them was looking up
at me. It was Smiley. The other one's back was
turned. I could see he had short dark hair.

Thanks to Luke's greeting, it was too late now
to try anything subtle. I walked over to the table
slowly, beer bottle dangling by the neck in my left

hand. I'd taken them once, but they might not be so easy a second time.

"Someone on a hog took a shot at me two hours ago on seventy-three. Either of you know anything about it?"

The short-haired clean-shaven one lifted a cut and bruised face up to me. He looked disappointed that mine wasn't.

"What would we know about a thing like that?" he asked. "We've been here for three hours. With a roomful of witnesses."

"How about Blackbeard? He been here?"

"Who?"

Smiley started sliding his chair back. I opened a space in my shirt and showed him the butt of the pistol. He stopped.

"Listen," I said. "You've tried to take me twice now, and you couldn't. You can't. Leave it before you get hurt."

Smiley started laughing. Shave-face joined him, but I didn't think his heart was really in it.

"I'm on to you. The cops are going to shut you down."

"The cops!" Smiley roared. "The cops ain't gonna do shit."

I thought about trying to beat it out of them, but I couldn't see how or where. I stood watching them laugh until they settled down to chuckles, then went back to the bar, put the bottle on it, and left. Luke was long gone.

I drove home. As soon as I got inside I called my one biker friend in Denver. He drives a school-bus down there and I caught him home between shifts.

"Ronny? This is Hank. I want a favor."

"Hey, Hank, how you been?"

"I've been busy. And I've been shot at by a guy riding a black Harley. I thought you might be able to help me find out who."

"No shit?"

"No shit."

"You got any idea why? Or were you just driving so slow you looked like a stop sign?" Ronny started laughing. He never did like my driving habits.

Lots of people, judging by the number of bullet holes, like to use road signs for target practice around Denver. It's pretty stupid and pretty dangerous to people living behind the signs. The damage tapers off rapidly two counties out in any direction. That says something to me about the cause.

But not many people shoot at other cars for the hell of it.

"I think it ties into the death of Bill Evans a while back. At least that's all I can put together."

"I read something about him in the paper, but we never rode together. Do you know what kind of a Harley the guy was on?"

"Nope, but I'm pretty sure it was a Harley. I got that much of a look at it."

"Yeah, but what kind? Was it a sportster or a panhead or what? We might be able to narrow it down if you knew what it was."

Ronny knew bikes. I didn't.

We met at the Westside Chop Shop on 14th Street, a gas station converted into a cycle store. There was a parts department, a no-nonsense, find-what-you-need outfit only grudgingly attached to a biker's Brookstone Tools sort of place, selling every chrome-plated accessory and knickknack it might be possible to bolt or weld onto a motorcycle. Ronny took me to the counter to have me thumb through an illustrated book of all the Harleys ever made. It didn't help.

"I didn't see the bike that well," I said.

"Then how do you know it was a hog?"

"The sound. What else makes that much noise?" I asked.

"Your truck," he said.

"Not with the muffler on, it doesn't."

"Hey, I got an idea. Do you remember the sound pretty good?"

"I've got a pretty good memory for sounds, but don't expect me to describe it to you."

"I won't. Let's go back to the repair shop and talk to Leonard, the mechanic, see if he'll let us fire up a few different bikes. Maybe you can pick out the right one."

"Wouldn't different exhaust systems change the sound?" I asked.

"Don't worry. You'll recognize the right one, if he's got one here."

Leonard was a short, beer-bellied, middle-aged biker with the scars and ground-in dirt on his hands to prove his expertise. I wouldn't want to cross any of these guys, but like most monomaniacs, as long as you stay on the right side of them, they're friendly and helpful enough.

Leonard trusted Ronny enough to let him at the choppers, providing he kept me from touching them. It was obvious I wasn't part of the in crowd here. I understood his attitude. I didn't look as if I knew the clutch from the brake and mostly I didn't. I also knew how much money most guys had invested in their machines and that an insignificant scratch in a paint job might set me back a thousand dollars. Maybe a nose reconstruction, too.

Ron fired up a sportster, but I knew right off that wasn't the engine. He tried an old suicide-clutch police model, but it was too smooth and quiet. He got Leonard's old knucklehead and something in the rhythm was right.

"Crank it up a little," I suggested. He goosed it. It sounded right.

"You sure?" he asked.

"Pretty sure, unless there's something else that sounds like that."

"Nothing else."

"How many of these are there around?"

"Not many in running condition."

Ron got off, and we went back to drop off the keys and thank Leonard.

"What's the right thing?" I asked. "Should I give him a few bucks?"

"Don't be an ass. He wouldn't have done it except as a favor to me. It's all covered, or it will be when you pay me back. You can start with a sandwich." We went for calzones at Classic Pizza on Broadway.

"I'll ask around and find out who's riding a chopped knucklehead, and you can look around for some trees for me. I need about three four-foot pines and a few aspens to transplant to make a screen, ten feet long or so."

Ron had a small house on the west end of Denver
and spent an occasional day landscaping and gar-
dening. It struck me as pretty odd when I first met
him, but he was the first biker I'd ever gotten to
know. Up until Ron, they were all stereotyped in
my mind. Ride. Drink. Fight. People are never as
simple as the stereotypes.

Since Ron hadn't brought up the fact that Leonard owned the right type of bike, I knew Leonard
wasn't a suspect. Not in Ronny's mind and there-
fore not in mine.

I got home around six and with nothing else lined
out, I grabbed a roll of surveyor's plastic tape and
the dog and went looking for the trees. The aspens
would be no problem. A few kicks on a sharpened
shovel and wrap them in burlap, but the dirt ball
on a four-foot pine should be about all one man can
do to pick up and put in a truck. A favor is a favor,
though.

I found a group of pines that needed thinning on
the flat pasture at the south end of the place and
marked two of them, then walked west, flagging
half a dozen aspens as I went, making sure the ones
I chose were free from disease and hadn't been too
badly chewed up by the elk. They like the new
growth and the bark as a spring tonic. The other
two pines I found near the west fence line. I wanted

four to give Ronny a little choice. Since the finding had gone quicker than I expected, there was still enough daylight to dig the trees and load them up. I got my truck, my shovels, and some burlap and baling wire, stopped to load topsoil to fill in the holes I was going to make, and got Ronny's trees out of the ground. If he was around in the evening, I wanted to drop them off and be done with driving into Denver for a while.

NINE

I TOOK MY TIME coming out of sleep next morning, remembering an uncomfortable task that had to be done. I took my time getting out of bed. I had to look in that black plastic bag. Shuddering with the memory of my dream at Abyss Lake, I grumped into some dirty clothes and went down to brew brains and make breakfast. It would be a worse job empty than full.

I finished off a whole pot of coffee and a cigarette before I could get myself moving. Finally I went out to the barn, got a long-handled pitchfork, and gingerly hooked the bag off the top of the manure pile.

It wasn't as bad as in the dream, but it was bad enough. The feeling was a lot different, seeing the forlorn bits of what were once such beautiful animals. Not sadness and foreboding. It just made me damned mad. I retied the bag, slung it back up on the pile, and drove into Cottonwood. I wanted to stop at Geist's to try to get Luke to say some more about Bill's "selling shit on the side."

Luke wasn't there when I arrived, but someone else I knew was: the poacher with a shave. He was dressed in a business suit this time though, pinstripes and all. His briefcase was on the store counter under a leather motorcycle jacket that needed repair.

"I can have it for you next Tuesday," Jim said.

"Fine," said the suit. He grabbed the briefcase, bumping into me deliberately on his way out. It didn't matter much to me. I would deal with him on heavier terms before it was over.

"Friend of yours?" Jim asked.

"We've met."

"I bet you have," he laughed.

"He wasn't wearing a suit then, though," I added.

"Uh huh. There's a lot of those guys around these days. Nine-to-five bikers. They wear their leathers weekends, but they're accountants and businessmen during the week. I don't much like them."

He paused and looked at the counter. "It's dishonest in a way, living a double life like that. And that one I wouldn't trust two feet."

"What's his name?"

"Mike Carson. He works somewhere in Denver. Real estate, I think."

Hot damn! A name for Riley.

"Coffee?" I offered.

"Yeah. Thanks."

When I came back, Luke was in the store. I think he sits in a secret observation post near Main Street, scouting, until he sees a friend or another likely prospect for a mooch.

"Where's mine?" he asked.

"I'm not psychic, Luke," I said. I gave him a dollar. "Get yourself one."

Jim and I sat down and sipped coffee until Luke came back. He leaned against a saddle and uncapped his, blew on it to cool it down. Coffee costs fifty cents. Luke didn't bother returning the change.

"Luke, can I talk to you about something?" I waded in.

His eyes shifted to Jim and back again.

"I didn't hear nothing," Jim said and opened a newspaper.

"You know you can trust him," I said to Luke, and he knew he could. Luke nodded okay.

"If a guy had some shit he wanted to sell…" I began.

Luke's eyes showed a monetary interest.

"Just suppose. Or if he wanted to buy something contraband, illegal, who would he go see?"

"What kind of shit?" he asked warily.

"The kind Bill Evans used to mess around with."

Luke looked as if I'd accused him of criminal activity. He glanced at Jim again, but Jim was studying his newspaper. Luke glared resentment at me, but he said, "The guy who just left here."

I was right about Luke keeping an eye on Main Street.

"Or else Todd Stevens," he added.

He gulped the rest of his coffee and left in a hurry.

"Help any?" Jim laid down his paper.

"I don't know. It surprised me. I can talk to one of the two. Stevens and I met on a friendly basis. See you later."

On the way to the HHC I decided not to be too open about what I was after. I'd already been in one fight.

"Is Todd around?" I asked Serene in the office.

"Just a minute and I'll see if he's available."

I watched her walk out to go to his office. She had a nice walk. I wondered if Stevens hired her for her office skills or something else. Stupid question.

Serene returned and said, "Go on up." She smiled. I smiled back. It isn't love that makes the world go round as much as the small flirtations.

"Hey, Hank Eston. How are you?" Todd said.

"Fine. And yourself?"

"Great. Just great. The old *chi* is flowing and my moon's ascending."

Ascendant, I thought. Ascendant, asshole. At least get your bullshit straight.

"How can I help you? Did you finally come for that free massage?" He studied me up and down and muttered, "Spleen."

"No, not yet, but sometime soon. I want to buy some herbs and stuff, Todd."

"Why don't you talk to Sue?"

"I'd rather not bother her these days. I figured you'd know where to get some. Local."

"What kind?"

"Sue said Bill was using something."

Todd looked at me a few seconds. "I didn't know that, but it isn't surprising, knowing Susie. Hmmm." He thumbed through a phone index on his desk. "Let's try Diane Meyer."

He dialed the number and looked up at me. "Diane? This is Todd Stevens. Yeah. How are you? Look, I'd like to send someone over to you, a friend of Sue Fenton's. Okay? Thanks."

He hung up and wrote down an address.

"All set. Diane ought to be able to help you. She's the main source for most of this town. Good luck."

I hadn't missed his change of manner. At first he had been the good old boy, glad to see me. At the end his speech was clipped and he was glad to be rid of me. I told him thanks, ogled Serene again on my way out, and headed for Diane Meyer, local doctor of traditional Chinese medicine.

Meyer's office was in her house, a redwood-and-glass contemporary in one of the subdivisions blighting what used to be fairly decent high meadow just outside of town. Forget the mountains or let the clouds lower enough to hide them and the T-Bar Estates could be anywhere in dis-urban United States. Modern houses on quarter-acre lots. Paved roads and streetlights. Burglar alarm stickers on the windows.

Hers was not as well groomed as those around it. Picking my way across a patch of native grass strewn with gravel meant to ease the way in winter, I came to the downstairs door and knocked. No response. I took the liberty of letting myself in quietly.

Beyond a coarsely finished front hall was the waiting room, an ordinary Western-style living room, but hung with Oriental scrolls and calligraphy. There was a floor-to-ceiling bookcase, which captured my attention, of course. I noted a room farther in, with a desk and computer and shelves filled with jars and urns, and a small hall with two closed doors. Quiet voices came from behind one of them.

I turned my attention back to the bookcase. It held the usual New Age things, *The Stone Monkey, Beyond the Brain, Planetary Herbology,* but more than half the books were in Chinese or Japanese, so I couldn't even read the titles. Some looked very old, silk-bound volumes, which probably held the answers to most of my questions. Three years with Berlitz maybe? Not even then, I'd bet. A door opened and I heard the rustling of clothing. I turned.

She was tall and pale, dressed in Santa Fe style, with long graying hair left loose. She wore tooled western boots and a long denim skirt with, I swear, petticoats. And lots of silver jewelry. Was this Diane Eagle-in-the-Nest Meyer? Somehow I didn't think so. The mouth was too hard set and the eyes dark and guarded against their own depth.

"Can I help you?" she asked.

"I'm Hank Eston," I told her. "Todd Stevens just called."

"Oh yes. What can I do for you?"

"I'm trying to buy a supply of an herb, I think it is, or a Chinese medicine of some sort. Billy Evans was taking it, I think."

"Why don't you get it from Sue?" she asked.

I caught a hint of a smile as she said it. A hunch. I decided to run with it. I lowered my eyes and said softly, "I'd, uh, I'd rather not."

She got control of the smile. "Something sexual?" she asked. The edge was off her voice, leaving an undertone of sympathy.

"On that order. I think it was a sort of grayish powder."

"Yes, it comes that way sometimes. I'll show you what I have."

There was a pause, during which she looked into my eyes most disconcertingly. There was more to this woman than I expected. Kells, I remembered, had said she was one of the real ones, one of the few who knew her stuff.

She turned and strode to the room with the computer and the jars. Her walk was straight and masculine, at odds with the costume.

She didn't go directly to the herbs, I saw, but first consulted a printed list hanging at the corner of one of the shelves. It took her a minute or two. She came back with two small clear glass vials, one containing a green paste, the other a tiny amount of the gray powder, almost empty.

She handed me the gray one. I pulled open the stopper and sniffed. No doubt about it. My left wisdom tooth cringed just as it had at Sue's.

"That one is for impotence," she said. "It's taken internally. The other is a topical mixture, for size and staying power."

That was a relief. I wondered how much embarrassment I would have to take. I gulped theatrically.

"It's the impotence," I mumbled.

"Unfortunately, I keep only a tiny amount of this on hand. It's for treating prostate problems mainly. This is a pure powder here, which has to be mixed with some other stuff to make the proper dosage. Actually, I seldom am consulted for such things. I'm rather surprised Todd would send you to me for it."

"Why is that?"

"Because lately I've been getting it from him instead of my source in San Francisco."

"All of your herbs?"

"Oh no, only that one. It's extremely rare and expensive, you see, and the dealer in Chinatown never really liked selling it to me anyway. A little taste of racial discrimination, perhaps."

"What's it called?"

"*Yu kuei wan.*"

"What does that mean?"

"Roughly, 'extra spirit cup.' It supplies surplus *chi* to the *yuan shen,* the right kidney, mainly in males."

"Is that the powder or the mixture?"

"The mixture."

"What's the powder called?"

"*Lu jung* or *lu shuangi,* usually. Sometimes *lu chiao jung* or *lu chiao shuang.*"

"What does that mean, exactly?"

"What's your real interest in this?" she asked.

I almost told her, but in the end it was still too thin, and I couldn't be sure she didn't have a part in it somewhere.

"Look," I said, "I'm a friend of Brian Kells. Would you write down the Chinese name for this, so I can take it to him and have him tell me? Would you trust him to decide if I can be told?"

She gave me another one of those long looks. I expected her to say "liver" or "kidney," but I guess that wasn't it. She went to a desk and stood, writing Chinese characters on a notepad. She tore the sheet off and handed it to me.

"It's delicate," she said. "Brian will understand."

"It's serious," I said. "I can't say more now."

Which, I suppose, meant that I pretty much trusted her after all. Anyway, she seemed to accept it. I gave her back the vial.

"You'll have to press Todd, I think," she said. "I have no idea where he gets it."

"Thanks. I'm sorry."

"I hope there will be no reason for you to be," she said.

So did I.

TEN

I CALLED KELLS from the 7-Eleven at the end of Diane Meyer's street to tell him I wanted some Chinese characters translated and got invited to drop by for dinner. I accepted and offered to bring the wine. Kells told me translating Chinese would be much more pleasant than reading the autopsy report he had for me. We left it at that until I got there.

I called Amos Johns after that. The phone rang a long time, but he finally answered.

"I'm moving pretty slow, but I'm moving," he said. "When you coming out?"

"Tomorrow?" I asked.

"No, I got to go to the doc's and then meet with some elders in Kittredge."

"Day after, then."

"Let's shoot for it. Call me before you come."

"Okay, I will. Bye."

On the way out of town I stopped at Cottonwood Liquors and bought a bottle of Chateau Ste. Michelle Riesling, my favorite white since the supply of cheap pre-Chernobyl Moselle dried up. The only thing good to come out of that mess; it lowered our imbalance of trade a little.

The sun was low, on what would have been the horizon if we had a horizon anywhere in the mountains. We get a long twilight instead. To get to Kells's place I had to go past my own place, then another mile up Branch Creek. By the time I got to the turn and started along the winding road that follows the creek, the shadows under the willows and cottonwoods were deep enough to need the headlights. I saw a few deer cross the road ahead, one a fawn still spotted. None with antlers.

It was cooling rapidly, too. I had to choose between a bit of chill and being able to listen to the creek bubbling with the windows down. I opted for the sound. I'd be warm soon enough.

There are a few other thirty-five acre parcels on Branch Creek. State law had once set that as a minimum subdivided plot outside town or city limits. I think that law is still on the books, but it generally doesn't count for a thing anymore. I don't know how Kells and the other owners in the Branch Creek area have staved off the developers so far, but I have little hope of their managing to do it forever.

Kells's driveway was marked by a mailbox with a street number in the thousands. It's narrow, curving, and bumpy. I understood why he didn't want to improve it, but it was a bitch to plow in the winter. I drove down the two hundred yards of it to the house. The light over the front door was on for me.

The house isn't much, a frame two-story with cedar siding, but Kells had added an extensive deck structure on two levels, the lower section of it wide, varnished redwood planks, smoothed and butted, to give him a surface for his martial arts exercises. I knew he had done karate, but now seemed devoted mainly to the Japanese sword. He did a lot of painting and Japanese calligraphy, but I had no idea how he made a living.

Monika Kells answered my knock and invited me in. She was wearing a leather mini, high heels, and a hell of a plunging neckline. I wondered if she usually dressed like that at home in the evenings, or whether it was just for company. Or just for me. It made me nervous. Kells's wife was way too sexy for a married woman of forty or fifty or however old she was. Incongruously, there was nothing at all seductive in her manner. Her devotion to Kells was unmistakable. Still, that's the sort of thing I never entirely believe in. Even more incongruous was that she worked for the Forest Service as a field inspector. She spent her days in jeans and boots.

"Well, look who's here," she said in her German-accented English. "Good to see you, Hank." She gave me a hug. I accept hugs from her.

"We're having martinis," she said. "Care to join us?"

"That's a little too strong for me," I told her, handing her the wine. "Have you got a beer?"

"Of course. Brian will be up in a minute. He's finishing some paperwork, I think. Have a seat."

I didn't want to sit, so I walked to the fireplace, poked at the fire to get it up a bit, and then looked for the hundredth time at the Japanese calligraphy over the mantle. It looked like a row of four childish drawings of dreams. Kells had told me it had been brushed by his sword teacher in Japan and said "A hundred polishings perfects the self." I guess so.

Monika brought my beer and we discussed mutual friends and baking herbal breads. I heard a door open and shut down the staircase, and Kells's tread on the carpeted stairs.

"Hullo, Eston," he said, with the accent on the name. He was wearing a Bavarian loden jacket and a shirt with a stand-up collar. He dresses in the evenings too. I don't.

"Welcome. Got a drink, have you? Good. Here's the report you wanted. Dinner's in…what, love?" he asked, turning to Monika.

"Oh, about fifteen minutes."

"Right, there you have it. Do you want me to look into your other matter now, or can it wait till after we've eaten?"

"Afterward will be fine," I told him. "Have you read this report yet?"

"Good heavens no. No education in the sciences at all. Western sciences. You're on your own there, I'm afraid."

He turned on a reading lamp next to an armchair, made sure I had a table with an ashtray and a coaster for my drink, and followed Monika into the kitchen, enjoying the view of the heels and mini. I sat down after enjoying it myself.

I'd need a medical dictionary to understand some of it, but it was clear enough to get the cause of death. Massive trauma to the right kidney resulting in internal hemorrhaging. Cause of trauma not determined.

"Cause unknown," I muttered. "The guy was beaten to death. He just didn't bleed out right away."

"Must you?" Kells called from the kitchen.

"Sorry."

I thought about it in silence. I suppose if they don't find a piece of tire iron stuck in a wound they can't say it was caused by a tire iron. No jumping to conclusions. It occurred to me that I might have been doing just that, but Sue said he told her he'd been in a fight. Didn't that prove it?

Well, maybe not quite.

I sipped the beer and became aware of aromas from the kitchen. Garlic. Lots of garlic, and herbs, and olive oil. My stomach spoke up. Monika was my kind of cook. Kells's too, obviously. I heard chatter and laughter. They were cooking together and having a good time doing it. I suddenly felt terribly lonely. There are drawbacks to bachelorhood, too.

Dinner was as good as it smelled, mackerel from the Granada Fish Market done up in a Greek-style garlic and lemon sauce, a rice pilaf, and a salad. There was nothing like that available at the Pines. We talked about Denver restaurants and environmental pollution. It didn't seem to spoil anyone's meal, and what I had to say to Kells wouldn't have gone down well at the dinner table.

Afterward, Kells made cappuccinos and brought out Montecruz cigars. Monika retired to the kitchen to wash dishes. I gave Kells the notepaper with Diane Meyer's Chinese characters on it.

"She called me about this," he said.

"What did she say?"

"That she wasn't certain whether you were impotent or were chaffing her." Kells made the same sort of little grin Diane Meyer had.

"So what did you tell her?" I was moderately pissed. I just couldn't see any of it as funny.

"I told her that knowing you, it was unlikely that either was the case. She explained somewhat her problem with all this, and if it proves to be what I think it is, I'll explain it to you as well. I may have to ask you for a promise of confidence."

He looked at the note. There's a full bookshelf above their dining table. He reached up and pulled down a Chinese dictionary.

"I'm not sure how to translate this character in a medical context," he said, pointing to a complicated squiggle of Meyer's. "One moment."

He thumbed through what appeared to be a sort of index of similar squiggles, said *mm* and *ah* once or twice, then read a paragraph next to a squiggle that looked like one of Meyer's squiggles.

"Right," he drawled. "Of course, I could probably have deduced it from the context. Okay. I've got it. Now I suppose I've got to decide whether I can tell you."

He sipped his espresso—no cappuccino for

him—and dragged on his cigar, looking at me as if he was about to say "liver" or "kidney." I was fairly sure he wouldn't. I realized suddenly that I didn't really like him, though I trusted him in general and valued him in some ways. I couldn't like him, though. He looked on people—on me—the same way he looked at wildlife. It just wasn't quite right.

"Look, Eston," he said at last, leaning forward and trying to lock my eye, "it's delicate. I've got very mixed feelings about this myself. It involves very reasonable Western laws and equally reasonable Oriental theory and practice. They clash. It's just not simple."

"Can you give me a hint?" I asked, even more pissed.

"I may be able to give you all of it," he said. "It is, after all, a matter of facts available in books in libraries. Diane and I are not harboring a secret. Would you consider describing to me why and how it is that you need to know this? Given that, on the whole I'd rather tell you myself, placing it in context, than have you dig it up as uninterpreted fact."

I hate the way Kells says the word fact. It sounds the way most people I know say dirt. Pissed as I was, I figured I could tell him what was going on. I'd eaten at his table and smoked his cigars, after all. I laid it out for him, all but where the black bag was. And the dream at Abyss Lake.

"Oh well, of course, then. Sorry to have been so slow," he said. "You're right on target, you know. *Lu jung* means 'deer powder,' as does *lu shuang*. The difference probably only has to do with how finely the powder is ground. The *chiao* of *lu chiao jung* or *shuang* means 'deer horn powder.' Spot on. Congratulations."

"So it's almost a literal translation except for the other deer parts. What happens to the penises?"

"Those go straight to China or Japan. Modern Western practitioners think their use is just superstitious. They don't recognize the importance of the antlers being taken in the velvet, either, while still growing, covered in fuzz and infused with the blood of the animal. In the East they do, and there's a hell of a premium placed on antlers in velvet."

He reached into the cabinet under the bookcase and pulled out a bottle of Jameson's and two shortstemmed glasses. I declined. He poured himself a finger. Monika came out of the kitchen, leaned down to give Kells a kiss on the cheek, dangerously opening the already transfixing blouse.

"I've got a disgustingly early morning," she said.

We rose and bid her thanks and good night.

Kells's eyes followed her out, revealing his weakness, I thought, or maybe not. Maybe he just saw her as wildlife, too.

He sipped his whiskey. "The amount of powdered antler needed to make the *jiao*, or any of the potions, is very small. There are in Japan, and probably in China, farms where tame deer are raised and the antlers can be removed in velvet without killing the animals. The penises are taken when the deer is older and ready to become meat anyway; it's just a matter of avoiding wastefulness at that point, just the way you save the Rocky Mountain oysters when you're making steers.

"The problem, of course, is greed. Men are greedy creatures, not only for money, but for long life and sexual prowess. Where an appropriate formula for curing prostate enlargement or impotence uses perhaps an ounce of powdered antler, a year's supply, say, a greedy man might take an ounce of it straight every night he spends with a girl he wants to impress. It's also one hell of an aphrodisiac, you see. Mixed in a *jiao*, a topical cream, it can enlarge the penis, significantly they say, a matter of at least as much importance to an Oriental male as to a Western one."

"Surprise, surprise. People are people even in the Orient," I said.

He slugged down the Jameson's in the glass and poured a good two fingers more. I could see he wasn't having an easy time with this. We had never been on the sort of terms that allowed for discussing sexual topics on the personal level. He and Monika had tried fixing me up with a succession of girls—Monika's Bavarian niece on visits, a new girl who had got on the staff at Monika's Forest Service office in Bradley—but they'd both had the grace not to ask me how things had gone. Also, Kells was a small guy, not quite five-eight, and while he was slim and fairly limber, he was not exactly a physical specimen. I suppose discussing it could be delicate for him, though I didn't think that's what he'd meant when he had used the word. Or what Diane had meant when she'd used it.

"The point is that there are laws, not only in the States but around the Eastern world, that are tough on the traffic in antlers, rhino horns, wild animal parts in general. Mostly they make sense. But in the terms of traditional Chinese medicine they force the responsible medical use of these substances underground, into the black market. That's why Diane's supplier in San Francisco's Chinatown is hesitant to sell her the stuff. All of it is illegal, even the stuff from domesticated deer. So how are legitimate doctors of Oriental medicine to treat patients who legitimately need it? You see the problem."

"But what's going on here has got to stop," I insisted.

"Certainly it does! It's disgusting, ugly, and unnecessary. It's just a matter of how you go about it, you see. It could lead to the destruction of serious, responsible doctors of Oriental medicine if it's not handled right. By the way, treatment of prostate cancer and its prevention has a significantly higher success rate through Chinese herbs and acupuncture than anything other than radical surgery. And Colorado has the highest rate of prostate cancer in the States. Do you want your arsehole reamed out one day?"

That brought a shiver. "I will take a drop of that Jameson's if you don't mind," I said.

"My pleasure," he said as he poured.

Now I knew why the deer were being mutilated. For profit. I should have known. It had to be stopped. That might even have to take a higher priority than seeing myself clear of Bill's murder. Stevens had to be in on it. I wasn't sure how to deal with it, and I was just fuzz-headed enough that it would have to wait until morning.

"That's all for tonight," I said. The whiskey was hitting me hard. I have no idea how a little guy like

Kells can pack away martinis, Riesling, and Jameson's the way he does. I sure as hell can't.

"Eston," he said as I was leaving, "would you arrange some way for me to meet Sue Fenton again? I'm curious about her study of *t'sui na* and kung fu. Do you think that would be a problem?"

"It shouldn't be," I told him. "I'll see what I can do."

That pissed me off again. More research, more observation of the wildlife. I would do what I could, though. I'd been drinking his whiskey.

Driving out his bumpy road, I knew one thing for sure. Tomorrow I'd see Todd Stevens again, and to hell with practitioners of traditional Chinese medicine.

ELEVEN

SUE CALLED AFTER I got home, asking me to get rid of Bill's possessions. His next of kin didn't want them, and she didn't want to deal with it or have the reminders of a bad experience around. There was quite a bit of furniture, she said, so I called Kells Wednesday morning to ask him if he could meet me in Cottonwood to give me a hand, mentioning that it might be the best opportunity he'd get to talk to Sue. I can be as practical a man as Amos Johns.

But it wasn't the best opportunity. She wasn't home when we got there with my truck the next morning. She'd left the door unlocked with a note taped to it.

"Sorry you missed Sue, Brian," I said, "but you can still help me with some of these things."

"I'll help and don't feel you've wasted my time," Kells said. "She did invite us to make ourselves at home. I may learn more from looking around her house than I would have from talking to her. Let me poke around for a few minutes.''

I went to the kitchen and checked the refrigerator for a can of pop. All she had was diet. My body can only handle natural, organic poisons. I found a beer and settled for that. I don't like to drink and work unless it's hard physical labor in hot weather. The alcohol slows me down and puts my mind into vacation mode, but I was thirsty, and chlorinated water doesn't cut it when you're accustomed to sweet well water. I found a couple of apples, too, and went outside to peel them with my pocketknife while Kells rooted around. The birds and squirrels would appreciate the scraps, and I wasn't worried about Kells appropriating anything. I didn't have any doubts about his integrity. It was something about his humanity that bothered me.

"An interesting bookshelf here, Eston," Kells called out from Sue's bedroom. "Not anything I studied in college, but a good assortment of New Age primers."

I went in and looked. It was mostly the same stuff Diane Meyer had. I picked up a copy of a paperback by someone named Siegel and skimmed through it. Lots of assumptions taken as gospel truth. Lots of foregone conclusions and self-supporting proofs. I put it back. Kells had gone into the bathroom and rummaged through the medicine cabinet and looked around the kitchen. He was standing in the living room, looking over Sue's charts while drinking a beer of his own.

"You never mentioned you knew someone interested in Chinese astrology," he said.

"I didn't know she was until I saw these things hanging here last week and asked her about them. Is the Oriental version any different from the American method? Or is it just different symbols?"

Kells wasn't paying much attention to what I was saying. He was reading the charts. He has a good mind for details, even the useless ones.

"Good calligraphy cannot be done with a pen," he muttered. "Sorry. What did you say?"

"Is the system different from Jeanne Dixon's or what's-her-name Goodman's?"

"Oh yes, entirely different. It's based on the lunar calendar, you know, Year of the Dragon and all that? Diane Meyer uses it, too, but doesn't make such an artistic thing of it. She's got it in a number code on her computer. It's an adjunct to a very sophisticated level of Chinese medicine. And Chinese martial arts as well, by the way. What sort of kung fu does Sue study?"

"I don't know," I told him. "Is it important?"

"It might be," he said. "I don't know yet."

He wandered over to look at her herb collection, like I did when I was here the last time. He picked up a prescription bottle, looked at the contents, then tossed it to me.

"Do you happen to know what these are for?"

I didn't. Furoxone. I'd never heard of it.

He put the bottle back on the shelf. "Well, it's time to move some furniture."

I finished my beer and put the empties in the trash. Bill's stuff added up to a decent load in my truck: bags of clothing and magazines, a dresser and two chairs, a footlocker, and a wooden table. I might have been able to sell it for a few bucks somewhere, but that somewhere would be in Denver, and I didn't feel like driving down there again. The good stuff would get recycled out of the county landfill by scavengers and I'd be done with it in less than an hour.

We finished the loading, shut Sue's door, and went to town. I bought lunch at Sue's expense at the local Chinese restaurant. Nothing fancy, but good enough and more than fairly priced. The management had added a nice extra touch that day, a light jasmine fragrance in the tea. Kells lectured me on Chinese culinary practice. Apparently they consider food the same as medicine and dine according to what ails them. I asked him if a craving for sweet and sour pork indicated what ailed you. He said it probably did, but he'd have to ask Diane just what ailment it indicated. I suggested it meant a shortage of sweet and sour pork in the system. That, to my amazement, made sense to him.

Kells and I said good-bye after lunch and I set off to take care of the day's second task. It saves gasoline to combine trips to town when it's possible.

Everyone's socks get dirty. Some of us have a mother. Some of us have a maid. I use a laundromat. I could rig up a washing machine at the ranch, but that would require forethought, and I've only been there a decade and a half. I drove past Kells in his car, thanked him again, and hauled my dirty laundry to Cottonwood's laundromat, where I stuffed it into two triple loaders, carefully sorted according to amount of dirt, rather than color. My method.

I loaded the machines with quarters, switched the dials to hot, hoping against odds to come up with at least lukewarm, and carefully dumped in what looked like plenty of soap. I pushed the coin slides home and made sure the machines started, then wandered to the bulletin board to see if anything I needed was up for sale. It wasn't, but I expected that. I turned and checked my fellow customers. A couple of unemployed carpenters from the look of them. A few frumpy housewives with bored children in tow and one pretty blonde. We smiled at each other. I walked over and sat down.

"I'm Hank Eston," I said.

"Didi Burnham. Nice to meet you finally," she said. "I see you around town, but we've never met."

"I spent summers here as a boy. Out past Pyrite Junction. Full-time I suppose I've lived here about a dozen years now, so that's possible. I look after my uncle's ranch."

"That must be nice, living on a ranch," she said.

"It is, all things considered. How about you?"

It's American tradition, defining a person by occupation, but then there isn't much weather in a laundromat and anyway, when it comes to the weather, I'm a stoic.

"I'm an astrologer," she said.

"Really. I have a friend who's gotten into that. Chinese astrology."

"Sue? You're that Hank?" she asked. "Sue's friend?"

I smiled. "I guess that Hank."

"Wow. We should talk, you know. About Sue. She's been a friend of mine for a long time."

"Well then, let's talk."

"Oh, not here, with all these people. Let's go to the Quiche and Carrot, okay?"

I sighed. Another vegetarian. I've never met a vegetarian I could get along with long-term. Hard, coarse accents, open-mouthed mastication, and vegetarianism had caused me to relegate half the women in town to my non-dating category, even if the women were attractive, which Didi was. I may be doomed to perpetual bachelorhood, but then there are worse fates.

"Sure, Didi," I said. "Let me run my wash and we'll go when you're ready."

"Aren't you going to dry them?" she asked. "I always do."

"My mother does it for me," I said.

"You live with your mother?" Her face showed extreme disappointment.

"Mother Nature," I said. "I hang 'em on a clothesline. Saves time. Saves gas. Saves money. Using a clothes dryer on a sunny Colorado day never made any sense to me."

I looked at the dials on my washers.

"Almost done. I'll get my clothes and meet you up there," I said, tapping her on the knee. She smiled and nodded yes and went to check her clothes in the dryers.

The Quiche and Carrot restaurant is one-half of

a lakeside establishment run by two brothers, native to the town, who, like many of the folks who don't commute to Denver, settled here after a disillusioning stint at college. The restaurant has a quiet, clean, sidewalk cafe atmosphere, serving strictly health food cuisine. I don't stop there much, but the Carrot side of the store is a well-stocked grocery where I pick up things of a quality I can't buy at the local chain store. They also carry the only commercial product that resembles real tomatoes I've ever bumped into.

I nodded hello to Eric, behind the counter, and told him I was waiting to meet someone, then sat down at a window table in the restaurant section. Eric came by, set two menus on the table and returned to his counter. Didi drove up and I enjoyed her walk to the door.

"This is much nicer," she said, sitting down opposite me. "I'm hungry. Let's order, then we can talk, okay?"

Eric came back.

"I'll just have coffee," I said, and looked up to see disgust on his face.

"I mean tea. Ah, Red Zinger."

"Not Red Zinger. Chamomile. And a bran muffin."

"Why?"

"Kidneys," he said.

He turned to Didi, and she ordered a tofu delight with sprouts and an organic root beer. He seemed to approve.

"How long have you known Sue?" she asked.

"About four years now. We met at a party. And you?"

"Almost two years. We were in the same women's support group. That's how we met, and we became super good friends. And I'm her personal astrologer."

Didi leaned toward me over the table, cupping her chin in her hands. Her voice got serious.

"That's why I wanted to talk to you about Sue. I want to help her get through all her pain, and I was told you're a friend and want to help her, too."

"That's true," I said, "but Sue isn't making it very easy to do, never being around to talk."

"Well, if you're serious about it," she searched my face to gauge my concern, "you ought to know some things about her."

She paused, looking at the tabletop, organizing her thoughts or coming to a decision of some sort about me. Her face set and she looked up.

"First, Sue was raised in Eastern Pennsylvania, in a small town, Phoenixburg. Her parents own a children's shop there, toys and clothing, and according to Sue, they had a good income. She had a happy middle-class upbringing so far as they were concerned.''

Another pause and look at the table.

''But Sue has an uncle, Uncle George, who was…well, he didn't help her any.''

I nodded and said nothing, letting her unravel it in her own time.

''Well, the gist of it is that George was a preacher, sort of, a hellfire-and-brimstone type, always citing scripture and trying to convert everyone around him to his type of Christianity. Sue's folks weren't interested, but that didn't stop George from trying all the time. It was sort of a family pastime, you know, to invite George over and listen to him rant and rave.

''Well. Sue always liked him, she said, but when she got into her teens, well…''

Didi studied the table again. I guessed this was the important part. It was. She blurted it out.

''Well, when Sue was fourteen her Uncle George came by one afternoon when she was home alone and raped her, spouting scripture right up to his orgasm, she told me.''

I studied the table now, compressing my lips, not knowing what to say.

''She'd never told anyone before. Not even her

parents. She just repressed it. The worst of it was that it continued all through high school. She'd try to avoid being alone with him, but he'd manage to catch her and put her through it again and again. He'd threatened her, of course, so she never told anyone. She just endured until she graduated. Then she left home.

"I didn't know," I said. "Sue never mentioned any of that."

"I know. She's never told anyone but me."

I shook my head in sympathy and in disgust.

"Enough about the past," Didi said. "Here comes our food."

We ate in silence. I thought about what Sue had been living with, trying to match some of her behavior patterns to this history. Some of it seemed to make a certain sense.

Didi was probably wondering if she'd been right to have told me. She finished and pushed her plate aside. I poured a second cup of tea.

"Sue isn't the only woman that's happened to, you know," she said.

I nodded again. This wasn't an easy conversation for me to be in. It was too easy to say the wrong thing.

"What really worries me is Sue's horoscope."

"How's that?" I asked.

"Well, her chart showed her past, sort of, but it's the future I'm talking about. It indicates that four accidents or injuries will happen to people close to Sue, her friends. One seems to be a severe head injury or maybe a death. Sue will be hurt even more by these misfortunes, I know."

"Didi, nothing personal, but I don't put a lot of stock in horoscopes. They're usually pretty vague, aren't they?"

"No. Not if they're done properly, and I do my charts properly. I predicted Mary Zurna's automobile accident last year, and it was accurate even to the color of the new car she got. Astrology works, even if you don't believe in it."

"Okay, okay. I'll trust you. Did you predict Bill Evans's death?" I asked.

"I'd consider that to be one of the misfortunes with her friends, wouldn't you?" Didi said.

"Yeah, I guess it qualifies."

Didi placed her hand on mine, searching my face again.

"Help her, Hank. Stay by her, won't you? She's under so much stress."

"I'll do what I can, Didi. She doesn't seem to want to talk to me much, but I'll keep an eye on her."

"Dear Hank," with a deep gaze into my eyes. If

she was about to say anything more it wouldn't be "liver" or "kidney."

"I'd better get going and hang out my clothes before they're mildewed."

She released my hand and I picked up the check. "I'll get this. We'll see each other again, I'm sure. Take it easy."

I paid and left the Quiche, heading for home, thinking about all that Didi had said. I got to thinking about the pills I'd seen at Sue's and about Didi's concern with the stress Sue was under. Didi obviously knew Sue better than I did.

I called up the Peaks Pharmacy in Cottonwood from a pay phone. All things considered, Didi's prediction of a head injury brought up images of suicide to me.

"Peaks Pharmacy, where your dollars go far, but you don't have to. James here."

"James, is this the pharmacy bench?" I asked.

"Yes it is. How may I help you?"

"If you're not too busy, could I get some information from you about a specific drug?"

"I'll try. What is the drug?"

"Furoxone," I said. "Is it a tranquilizer? A sleeping pill? What's it prescribed for?"

"Furoxone. Why do you ask?"

"Curiosity," I said. "A friend of mine is taking

them and, well, I'm a little concerned about a possible overdose. Not a lot, just a little.''

"All right. One moment.''

I heard him punching it into his computer.

"Here it is,'' James said. "You needn't be concerned. Furoxone is a specific for dysentery, and for the parasite *Giardia lamblia.* Do you know what that is?''

"They're the same, aren't they?''

"No. Dysentery is caused by an amoeba. *Giardia* is a protozoan often found in beaver feces and in surface water here in the mountains. Anyway, the only danger from an overdose would be nausea, maybe a headache or a rash. Uncomfortable, but not dangerous.''

"Thank you.''

"You're welcome. Please let us be of service when you need a pharmacy.''

That was a relief.

Afternoon thunderstorms were building up. It was a crapshoot as to whether my laundry would get a final rinse before it dried.

TWELVE

I HAD JUST ABOUT finished hanging the laundry when I heard the phone ringing. I sprinted through my door and caught it before it quit.

"Eston."

"Hank? This is Ronny. Got a pencil?"

"Hang on." I caught my breath and found a pen and an empty envelope on the dining table.

"I just got in, sorry." I took a few more breaths.

"I found three names for you in your neck of the woods. Check 'em out. One of them rode with Billy, a guy named Don. But you know, that guy could have been from anywhere. Some folks are just crazy and'll shoot something for the hell of it. Maybe he doesn't like blue trucks."

"Maybe. Give me the names, Ron, and I'll check them out tomorrow."

I wrote down the names and addresses: Jim Swanson on Briar Lane, Don Lorenz on Hilltop, and Jack Wilhelm on Lakeside.

"Hey, I know the Wilhelms," I said. "Insurance people in Cottonwood. We bred our dogs last fall. He didn't have a beard then."

"They grow," he said.

"He's got light hair."

"They sell hair dye. As least you have two more to run down."

"Thanks Ronny."

"Welcome. Thanks for the trees. They're looking fine. Want to borrow a bulletproof vest?" he asked.

"No, I don't want to get that paranoid. Besides, its summer and those things are hot as hell to wear."

"Suit yourself. Let me know how it turns out or if I can help. Good night."

I went back out and finished hanging the jeans and towels. The early evening thunderstorm had passed. Lightning still glowed in clouds to the east. I walked the dog and checked on the horses, enjoying the moonlight and the sweet freshness of the rain-washed air. Then I went in, cleaned up, and turned in for the night.

Next morning over breakfast I checked a map to find Briar Lane. Hilltop, I knew, was in Piñon Park, Cottonwood's last low-rent district being squeezed between the country club and Los Piños housing development. Working-class housing was getting scarce in the area. "Scrub my floors, then disappear until next week" seemed to be the prevalent attitude among the Cottonwood elite.

Briar Lane was an old dirt road, only recently given a name, out my way. I thought I'd check it first, on my way into town. I set my dishes in the sink and took Musashi with me while I put out grain for the horses. It looked to be a hot day, so I put the dog back in the house and left the ranch.

Swanson, it turned out, was home. He worked nights in Denver and had been sleeping until I drove up and his dogs began barking. I explained that someone had told me he had an old knucklehead Harley he might want to sell. He was redhaired and a lot bigger than the guy I remembered shooting at me.

"Well, I don't," he said.

"Not even if the price was right?" I asked.

He gave me a cold stare, scratched his beard, and stretched leisurely. Then he turned and walked to his garage, motioning me to follow. When he opened the door I saw a bright red bike, torn apart almost piece by piece, occupying half of the garage.

"How much?" he asked, smiling broadly.

"Uh, that's a little more work than I want to get into, I think," I said.

"Right. Me too. Now let me get back to sleep, will you?"

I apologized and drove to Cottonwood. One down. I went past the Wilhelms' for the sake of being thorough. No one was home, but I could see the bike. It was glossy black, but I would have recognized Wilhelm. And he never seemed homicidal to me. Fanatical about Republican politics, but not homicidal.

Lorenz's bike wasn't anywhere I could see, and I thought I'd have to come back, but I didn't. One of the neighbors came out to find out what I was doing. I gave her the same story I'd given Swanson.

"I don't think he'd want to sell it. It's his pride and joy," she said.

"Well, what color is it, anyway?"

"It's white," she told me.

So much for that. Maybe Ronny was right and it wasn't anyone local. I'd just have to be careful until something more turned up. More afternoon storm clouds were building up, hovering in the peaks. It was past time to see Stevens again.

I ARRIVED AT THE HHC just in time to see Sue come barreling out of the office, fists clenched and cursing under her breath.

"Hi, Sue," I said as she approached. "Bye,

Sue," as she went past. I watched her drive off, then turned to go in. Stevens was leaning in the doorway, bent over and rubbing his back.

"That little bitch," he said.

"What happened? I don't think I ever really saw Sue's temper before."

"She was giving me a treatment and we were talking and suddenly she did something that hurt like hell. Hey, look at my back, will you? It sure is sore." He pulled his shirt up and I inspected the bruise.

"You'll have a black-and-blue spot, just below your ribs, but it doesn't look like much," I said. "What got her so riled up?"

"Business and things. One of her clients, Bill's death. I was trying to facilitate her emotional healing."

Bullshit even now. "You must have touched a sore point with her somewhere," I said.

"I guess so, but I had to do something. People are getting uncomfortable about Sue being around so much death and violence. I told her so and I told her I thought maybe she didn't handle the Bill thing the right way."

He paused.

"I mean, maybe she should have taken him to a hospital right away," he added quickly.

He wasn't telling me all of it. It sounded as if he'd accused Sue of being responsible for Bill's death. That didn't seem to be an efficient way to help someone get over their grief. I told him so.

"Well, maybe not. Maybe I did get a little heavy."

He eased himself straight, stuffed his shirt into his belt, groaned a few times and settled himself into a chair behind the front desk. I sat in one facing him. He squinted at me as if it had just occurred to him I was there. The red went out of his face and his breathing slowed. He laid his head on folded arms.

He sat up straight and slowly pulled open a desk drawer and took out a bottle of pills. He examined it, deciding whether to take one.

"Why are you here? Did you go to see Diane?" he asked.

"Yeah. She said that what I wanted would have to come from you."

"And what's that?"

"*Lu chiao jung, lu chiao shuang*, however you want to say it," I said.

"Didn't she have any on hand?"

"A little, not even a quarter of an ounce. She sent me back to you."

He looked at his pill bottle again, opened it, and

took a pill. I read the label. Nardil, an antidepressant. It was in the name of S. Williams.

"Is that a problem?" I asked after he got the bottle closed and back into the drawer.

"How much do you want? It'll take a day or two."

"A couple of ounces ought to do me."

"Do you know how much that's going to cost?"

I shrugged. "Give me fifty bucks' worth of the unmixed stuff, then."

He started playing with a letter opener on his desk. It had the Kiwanis Club seal on it.

He knew I knew. I wanted to give him hell and demand to know the names of his accomplices, but then I thought about the personal risks. I didn't want to end up in another fight, or in the morgue.

"Come see me tomorrow morning," he said.

I decided Sue's side of their little argument might be worth hearing, so I went into town to call her. Her answering machine kicked in and went all the way through the garbage routine. I suspected she might be at home, but monitoring her calls. After the beep I said, "Sue, if you're there, this is Hank. I want to talk to you."

There was a click, then Sue said, "Hi, Hank. I'm sorry. I just got in. Sorry about what happened at the center. I was just so burned up."

"What happened?"

"He accused me of causing Bill's death, said I should have called an ambulance the night before. Just because I take care of Amos Johns. And Didi and her damned horoscopes…"

"What did you do to him?" I asked.

"I hit him," she said.

"Why?"

"He had it coming."

"That's not like you, Sue," I said. And neither were her voice and shortened speech pattern. She usually rambled. Maybe she was still upset. "You want to talk about it?"

"No. Not now. Maybe later. Good-bye, Hank."

The lady sure didn't want to talk to me. I dropped in another quarter and dialed Amos Johns's number. The line crackled. I heard thunder, not too far to the west. The phone gave a snap and a hiss and stopped ringing. The dial tone returned reluctantly and I heard my quarter drop into the box. I considered forgetting about asking Amos to front for me and just giving Riley a call, but my gut warned me against it.

The thunder was louder and the front edge of the clouds darkened Main Street in patches. I pulled out my wallet as if I might find a clue in it, an idea of what to do next. I checked my cash. Less than fifty bucks. If I was going to buy powdered deer horn from Stevens in the morning, the next stop was the bank.

I crossed the street to the ATM and pulled fifty out of a dwindling account. That eight bucks I'd made off the Harrisons' water pump was the only money I'd earned in a longtime.

Lightning hissed over the hill north of Main, and the thunder came after it like a gunshot. The rain started with drops big enough to fill shot glasses. I sprinted back across the street and down a block to Geist's. There wasn't time to stop for coffee next door; it was coming down in sheets before the door closed behind me.

"Timing," Jim said. He was alone behind the counter, carving a spur leather.

"Sorry I didn't have time to stop for coffee."

"That's what I meant by timing. Speaking further of which, you know the auction's in four days."

"Damn, I forgot all about it. No sweat, though, I've got everything ready, the chutes oiled and all." Jim would go to Greeley before dawn on Monday, buy the cattle, and truck them up to the ranch by noon the next day or a little earlier. Four days. I sank down onto a saddle slung over a low sawhorse. It just seemed like too much.

"I guess Luke and I can handle it, if you're too busy," he said. He didn't look up from his carving.

I tried to figure if I had enough to go to Riley, if I had to get to Amos, if there was any way at all I could be out of the whole damned business in four days. There was no way to know. Come cattle day I'd just have to drop it. Cattle day and a while after.

"I'll be there," I told him.

I asked for any info he could give me about the North Cottonwood Freight Company, where Bill had worked.

"They're just a little outfit," he told me, "making local pickups and deliveries, running into Denver and once in a while as far as Colorado Springs or Fort Collins. Five or six vans and one or two semis, I think."

"Listen, Jim, could you do me a favor? I'd like to borrow your car for a few hours."

"Truck in the shop?"

"Never. You know I do my own repairs."

"Sure, you can have it. I've got the Jeep today. It's parked over in the lot, down by the creek."

The rain was down to a light mist. Jim gave me his keys and told me where the trucking company was. I left.

North Cottonwood occupied a run-down metal Quonset hut stuck on the hillside behind the premix concrete plant. A few fuel pumps, an outdoor grease pit, and an oil-soaked dirt parking lot. The employees matched their surroundings, but the trucks were clean and appeared nearly new. I parked close to the concrete plant and sat in the car, thinking of how to approach this crew. I was pretty sure the cops had been all over them for a while after the murder. Sue had said he'd been beaten by the guys he worked with, but I figured that wasn't this bunch necessarily. I was wearing a western shirt and fairly clean jeans. I guessed I could pass as a writer.

I drove into their parking lot, got out, and walked over to the open garage door. I stood waiting until a guy in coveralls, greasing the big rig, looked up and saw me.

I smiled and walked over to him. He was wiping the grease from his hands. I put my right hand out for a handshake.

"Hank Eston," I said.

"Jerry Bonner. What can I do for you?"

"I'm doing a little follow-up article, free-lance, for the valley rag, about Billy Evans. I'm a friend of his girlfriend, Sue Fenton, and since he worked here I thought I'd stop by."

"Yeah, the cops have been here too, a bunch of times. They ran a piss-poor nighttime surveillance out of those unmarked Fords for a while. You could see their binoculars flashing in the moonlight. Bill was a night mechanic. We run the trucks all day, so usually the repair and maintenance gets done at night."

He jerked his thumb at the semi. "I'm just finishing this one up. They swapped wheel bearings last night."

"That must be a job and a half on one of these babies. What's one of these wheels weigh?"

He ignored the question. I walked to the driver's rear dual.

"Did you know Bill?" I asked.

"Naw. I signed on after he was gone. The other night mechanic would know about him, but Don doesn't come in until six. Bill must have been a real clown, though."

"Why's that?"

"Little stuff. Like maintenance records. I went through 'em pretty good when I came on here. It was okay, I guess, 'cause there wasn't any trouble with any of the trucks that I could see, but the mileage figures didn't match up for the little vans. They'd get real good mileage on some days and normal mileage on the days in between. Ten, sometimes twenty percent difference. Maybe he was working on some kind of invention. Maybe he was just a screw-up with numbers."

"Could be."

I thought about that. The only times my mileage varied much was when the speedometer was broken and I had to estimate the miles driven. Or when I'd forgotten a tank of gas I'd put in.

"How many miles do you put on a van in a normal day?" I asked.

"Oh, five, maybe six hundred, max."

I felt my lips twist as I nodded. He didn't seem to notice. "Well, if you didn't work with him, how about the drivers?"

"I think they were all here when he worked here."

"Thanks."

I went into the office to ask around, but the drivers worked days. Bill had worked nights, so I didn't get much from the two that were there. The dispatcher told me something, though.

"We never had any trouble with Bill. He was a good mechanic and did his work on schedule. He had the run of the place and nothing ever disappeared. Not a tool, not a part, not a gallon of gas. That's unusual.

"No, wait, I take that back. He messed up a book of bills of lading one night. Spilled coffee or something all over them."

"Bills of lading. Loading tickets?"

"Yeah. You got to fill one out for every pickup and delivery. They're numbered."

I considered that a second. "What happened to them? Did you toss them out?"

"Hell, I can't remember. That must have been four or five months ago. I think he just chucked them in the garbage. No big deal. We buy them a case at a time. Yeah, Bill was a good guy. We never had a lick of trouble with him. Too bad what happened, ain't it?"

"It sure is. Hey, thanks for your time."

"No problem."

That was simple enough. Now to find out about Sue's training for Kells, though what that had to do with anything I sure didn't know. I stopped at a booth outside the Hamburger Haven near the trucking company to call her. While it was ringing I noticed what a good view you got of the garage from there.

She answered, to my amazement.

"Sue. It's Hank."

"Oh, Hank, I'm so glad you called. What are you doing now?"

What was this? I expect "Oh, you again" and get a come-on.

"Uh, nothing, I guess."

"Come over here right now," she said, her voice down in her throat. "Massage time."

"I don't know about the massage, but I'll come over."

"Make it soon, Hank."

"Okay. Ten minutes."

Too weird. Entirely too weird. I drove down to Main Street, parked Jim's Jeep, returned his keys, and walked up the hill to Sue's. It took a lot more than ten minutes. I felt I needed all the time I could get.

THIRTEEN

I HADN'T CLEARED my mind at all by the time I
knocked on Sue's door. I thought I heard water running inside, but I knocked again to make sure.
When she didn't answer after about a minute I tried
the latch. It was unlocked.

"Sue?" I called.

The water stopped running.

"Sue, it's Hank," I called again.

"Oh, Hank. In the shower. Make yourself at
home. I'll be right out."

I remembered one of the reasons I'd split with
her. Her showers always lasted twice as long as
anyone else's, a real fault in an area where wells
run dry.

She came out of the bathroom still damp,
wrapped in a towel and pulling her hair into a ponytail. With her arms raised and their muscles ro-
tating, her breasts rose above the knot in front.
There were droplets of water moving slowly down

between them. At that point I remembered the main
reason I'd got mixed up with her. Gonads.

"Remember the horoscope I was going to do for
you?" she asked.

"Oh yeah, I remember."

"It's finished. I'll show it to you in a minute."

She got the ponytail done and went to the
kitchen, swinging it just a little more than was natural. The towel barely left her buttocks in shadow.
She brought back a beer for me.

"Sit down and drink this while I get the horoscope."

"Thanks." It looked like she wasn't planning to
get dressed. I took a long pull from the bottle.

She brought in the horoscope and a handsome
tube for it. I have to admit it was beautiful. Kells
had not been impressed with her Chinese writing—
she did it with flat pens instead of a brush—but
even he had admired the work as a whole.

"Thank you, Sue. It's wonderful."

"I'd hoped you'd like it," she said. She rolled it
carefully and slipped it into the tube. "Will you
hang it in your cabin?"

"Of course I will."

She bent for a kiss. I took it on the cheek and
gave her a peck in return. I could tell she was disappointed, but I just wasn't willing to go through

all that again, especially after the string of strangers since me and up to Billy. It wouldn't fly, tits and ass notwithstanding.

"Sue, can you tell me the style of massage therapy you do?"

"*T'sui na,* mainly. *Wu hsing t'sui na.* Don't you have one of my cards?"

She gave me one. Why hadn't Kells thought of that?

"Do you still study kung fu from the same teacher, what's-his-name?"

"Ling. Sifu Ling. Yes, of course I do. And you. Has anything changed in your life?"

"No, same old stuff. Odd jobs, firewood, and cattle."

I was finished talking, finished being there. I'd got what Kells needed and I just wanted out. I'll admit it. The whole thing hurt.

There was no way out without a hug, maddening with that moist, scented skin wrapped in a towel, but I got through it and fled.

I drove home feeling pretty upset. A lot of guys I know would just have grabbed the piece of ass and never given it a thought, at least not until the sores started showing up or the blood count started going bad. The sixties are sure as hell over. I knew there was more to it than that, but it was just a gut feeling, and I had too much going on to give it any time. I let it go and put my mind on North Cottonwood Freight.

Bill got beaten up at night, when, according to the people working there, there was only Bill and one other guy there, Don Lorenz, a fellow biker. I wished I'd had the name Lorenz and a face from the trio on Amos's hillside connected. The antler-poaching gang had to figure into it, unless I had missed something serious somewhere along the line. Then I thought about what the mechanic had said about variations in gas mileage and missing bills of lading. They were using the trucks without the owners' knowing, presumably to transport something, probably something illegal.

When I got home I let the dog out and tossed a stick for him for a few minutes, then fed him and had a fast dinner myself. It looked like another long stretch in the house for the Moose, but that's the life of an American dog. Play and sleep. I had work to do.

My uncle kept a car in a shed near the cattle pens, an old Pontiac station wagon. I took a spare battery out of the barn, a case of oil, and some other such possibles, and drove the truck up there to get the car going. It took an hour. The carburetor was gunked and the fuel line clogged, but I got her going. I drove the truck back to the cabin and got a pair of binoculars, Navy surplus night surveillance seven-by-fifties, polarized monsters a deputy had left behind on a call years ago. I'd given them a phone call and a chance to pick them up, but I guess they didn't want them.

I locked up and walked back to the car, drove to Cottonwood, and parked near the freight company, where the side road intersects the main highway, so I could watch what went on nights at the daytime trucking company.

Not much happened for a long while. Trucks got washed and cleaned out, greased. One was driven inside the building for a few hours. I was getting bored and I wanted some coffee, but a stakeout's a stakeout. Then I remembered the burger blight that sits near the grocery store, half a mile away. I could drive there, keeping an eye on the freight office in my mirror. If I was careful, I would see any traffic come and go out of the restaurant window. I ordered a cup of styrene and a fried apple pie that looked suspiciously similar to their breakfast hash browns, but tasted artificially different.

Around ten o'clock I watched one of the small vans pull out of the freight lot. No one had gone into the lot, and one of the mechanics was still there, greasing another truck.

The van pulled out and headed for town. I ditched my coffee and ran for the car, then followed the van until it turned into a dead end, Granite Way. I couldn't follow it there without being seen, but there weren't many houses down that road. I'd check them out another time. The mechanic might be road-testing his repairs and having dinner on the way, or visiting a girlfriend on company time, but I didn't think so. Chances were good he'd return the way he came. The other direction, south, was the least direct route to just about anywhere. I went back to town figuring to pick him up as he came through.

I had to wait about an hour until the van came by. I started the engine and waited for him to round a hill so he wouldn't see me pull out. Or see me run the town's only red light. I pissed off a few other drivers when I ran it, but I didn't want to lose him. I never claimed to be a perfect gentleman.

It was a surprise, but not too much of one, when the van went past the turnoff to the freight company and headed for the interstate into Denver. I kept back half a mile down the hill past the truck safety runoff at Mount Vernon Canyon and followed him all the way to the Stapleton Airport turn. The driver headed for the freight entrance on a side road. I couldn't follow without being obvious. Cars don't often enter the freight gates except at shift changes. I pulled over near the maintenance hangars entrance and picked up my binoculars. The van stopped at the gate and handed out some papers, which the guard inspected. The guard went into his hut and wrote something in a book and on the papers, then came back to the van. He and the driver talked a minute. The guard handed back the papers and waved the van through. I watched until it disappeared around the corner of a building.

I put the glasses down and thought for a minute. The freight company supposedly ran only daytime. Maybe this was a special case, or maybe it was the reason Bill got beaten to death. I had an idea.

I drove away from the airport, southeast, looking for a drugstore or someplace I could buy a box and some wrapping paper. I passed a lot of car rental agencies and a few trucking companies—airports don't make nice, quiet neighbors for the upwardly mobile middle class—before I found an outpost of retail commerce, a five-and-dime store picketed at the end of a littered parking lot in a poor neighborhood. It was still open though, and that was the important thing.

I locked the car doors; even an old beater might not be too safe, sitting all alone out there. I couldn't find any shipping boxes, but I bought two large padded mailing bags and some shipping labels. And a pen. Back in the car I tore a piece off one bag and sealed it inside the other, put a label on the front, and wrote the North Cottonwood Freight Company's return address in the upper left corner of the label. Then I drove back to the gate.

The guard stood up when I stopped, but couldn't quite tear himself away from whatever was on his TV set just then. I waited patiently until he came out. I could hear canned laughter from the TV.

"Yeah, what's up?"

"North Cottonwood Freight sent me down. Their van driver left short one package and it's got to go with tonight's shipment," I said.

"Okay, so go on in."

"I just started on this job. I don't know where to go with it."

"Just a minute." He went into his shack and returned with a clipboard.

"Let's see. You just missed him. In a white van, right?"

"Yeah, a white van."

"He's logged in with a shipment of extruded plastics for Eastern Rim Enterprises, Seattle, going out on Overnight Freight flight 412."

I scribbled ERE, Seattle, on the shipping label while the guard put his clipboard back inside.

"That's him. How do I get there?"

The TV had captured the guard again. "Go around this first building," he said without looking at me, his face about a foot from his set's screen, canted like a first-grader over a writing tablet working on a "see Dick run" composition. "Then hang a left and go about four blocks. It's the second red brick hangar on the right. You'll see the sign."

"Thanks. How often does North Cottonwood make this run?" I yelled.

"Every other night," he said and waved me through without looking up.

I figure with security like that, a guy would have a tough time smuggling more than two elephants at a time onto airport grounds. I drove just far enough to get a glimpse of the van being unloaded near an Overnight jet and then headed back out. I stopped at the gate and honked. The guard waved me through, head still glued to his TV. I went home to bed.

FOURTEEN

I TRIED TO THINK of a way to track the sender of the shipment going to ERE. I was pretty sure North Cottonwood Freight wouldn't have a record of anybody on Granite Way. First thing in the morning I called the freight office and asked about having something picked up and delivered at night. The manager remembered me.

"Couldn't it be done during the day? We don't run at night."

"No. Production routine."

"I'm sorry, we can't help you. Try Fed Ex or UPS. It'll cost you plenty, but they'll help you out."

"While I've got you on the line, would you do me a favor?" I didn't wait for his response. "Could you tell me Don's home phone number? And the other mechanic's, too?"

"What for?"

"I'm still working on that article about Bill, remember?"

"Oh yeah. Sure, just a minute."

I wrote them down and thanked him. I looked in the local phone book, but couldn't find what I wanted. I called a woman I know at a realty company.

"Carrie, I need a favor."

"For you, sweetie, anything."

"Do you have a crisscross directory for Cottonwood there?"

"Of course we do."

"Look up a couple of numbers and let me have the addresses, will you?"

Neither number was on Granite Way.

"Look up Granite Way and give me the listings on it. Names and numbers."

"The entire street?" she asked.

"It's only about five buildings long."

She gave them to me. I told her she had a big dinner coming next time I was flush. She didn't refuse, but we didn't set a definite date, either.

Neither mechanic lived on Granite Way, and if the van driver was visiting anyone female there, it was someone else's wife. I tried calling both mechanics, but didn't get an answer.

It was almost noon before I got to Todd's office to pick up the stuff. Todd wasn't there. Serene told me Sue had called to apologize for yesterday's incident and had invited Todd to lunch at her house. I told her I'd catch him there and left.

Stevens's Subaru was parked in Sue's driveway when I arrived. Sue let me in with a kiss and a nervous smile. Todd had his mouth full, so we just nodded to each other. I noticed there was barely enough food for two and turned down Sue's offer to have lunch with them. Besides, I wasn't a Limburger cream fan, though the Paulaner Hefe Weisser, a heavily yeasted wheat beer, sounded good. It seemed an odd menu for Todd, with his high blood pressure, but a taste for that sort of thing had probably caused it in the first place. Sue drank wine when she drank anything alcoholic, so the beer had to be something special for Todd.

"I just dropped by to talk with Todd for a minute."

"Can't you stay, at least a little while?" Sue asked. She didn't look at me. The subtext read, "Don't."

"No, thanks. I've got a busy day today."

Todd held up two fingers to tell me he'd be over as soon as he swallowed. I looked over Sue's charts again. Bill's was gone, but I noticed one for Amos Johns hanging there, and a copy of mine. Todd's chart was on the couch. Lunch and stress relief session. There was a heavy air in the place, and not just from the Limburger.

Todd came over, wiping his mouth and beard with his fingers, and said, "I've got the stuff packaged. I'll be back in the office around two. Why don't you meet me there? Sorry, but Sue called me and, you know."

Yeah, I knew. "Well, thanks. Sorry to interrupt you two."

"No bother," Sue said. "Come back, Hank."

It bothered me. The whole scene there had me disgusted.

I used the time to check out Granite Way and then have some lunch.

There was no sign of a plastics extrusion outfit or any sort of commercial activity at the first two places. I could tell by the pine needles and grass growing in the third driveway that no one had been into it with a truck lately. The fourth place had tree branches hanging so low over the drive that only a sports car could have gotten up to the house. That left an old, empty garage dug into a hillside.

It was dilapidated, but the side-swinging wooden plank doors had been repaired and fitted with a lock, and there were tire tracks leading up to it. No house to go with it, but there was a path going up and over the hill behind it.

I followed the path, which passed through some trees and around a granite outcropping. I could see Cottonwood Lake, and then the Wilhelms' house at the end of the path. I'd forgotten about them. Subdivisions make me lose my bearings and focus my sense of location on roads, not the topography. That's always a mistake in this country.

I drove to Main Street and called the county assessor from the pay phone in the Pines.

"Can I find out who owns a particular piece of property?" I asked.

"Certainly. All I need is the property's legal description and I'll be happy to look it up for you," she said.

"It's 49173 Granite Way, in Cottonwood."

"No, no. That's not the legal description, that's the address. I need the legal description."

I closed my eyes and inhaled, deeply. If the county was so gung ho about street numbers, why the hell didn't they use them themselves? I let my breath out slowly and changed my attitude. I'd need patience dealing with the bureaucracy.

"Sir? Are you there?"

"I'm here. Sorry. Is there any way to cross-reference a street number?" I asked.

"Well, there is. Let's see. Where is that address, sir?"

I told her.

"Let me open my map book," she said. I could hear pages rustling.

"Here's Cottonwood. And Granite Way. It's a dead end southwest of Main Street, isn't it?"

"That's it. It's only a few hundred yards long."

"Yes sir. Let me put you on hold one moment and I'll look it up for you."

"Thank you," I said and drew another deep breath. I'd listened to too much "sir" for me. I'll use it to emphasize a statement or cool off a situation by assuaging a bruised ego, or to bruise an ego that needs it, but I'd certainly never been knighted.

"I'm sorry to keep you waiting, sir, but you see, we're required by law to use township and range or surveyed subdivision descriptions. It's a mess in the foothills."

"Yes, I know," I said. "Thanks for your trouble."

"That land is owned by Jack and Kate Wilhelm of 10217 Lakeview Drive, sir, in Cottonwood. Is there anything else?"

Yeah. I wanted to ask why one end of a piece of ground was numbered 49173 and the other end was 10217. Instead I told her no and hung up after thanking her again, but before she got a chance to say "sir" one more time. I sat down and ordered lunch.

I was waiting for my pie when I heard sirens. An ambulance and a sheriff's deputy went past, followed by an Animal Control truck with emergency lights flashing. That made a strange procession, unless someone's kid had been attacked by dogs. Maybe the dogcatcher was a coincidence. I hoped so.

I finished lunch and checked the clock. It was getting close to two. I drove to the Holistic Health Center to meet Todd.

"He went out jogging," Serene told me. "He's been getting self-conscious about his weight lately. Some of the practitioners have been kidding him about it."

"You mean the young girls aren't falling for him as fast as they used to. I'd say he could stand to lose a few pounds, regain his girlish figure."

I gave Serene my best lecherous smile. She took it in the mood it was more or less intended. She looked at the clock.

"Todd should have been back by now. He was only going to run around the lake. His legs were feeling cramped and he just wanted to stretch them out. It worries me. He took a pill before he left."

"Maybe I can go and find him," I said. If I

stayed much longer I was going to end up asking
Serene out and I didn't want to complicate things.

"He always goes to his house first," she told me.
"He rents the cabin from the Wilhelms and lets
their dogs out to run with him. Do you know where
that is?"

"As it happens, yes I do," I told her.

I headed for the lake, half a mile away, enjoying
the walk and the scenery. I took a short cut up over
a hill and dropped down to the shore, following it
around a few bends, and found out where the dogcatcher was headed. Same place as the ambulance
and the sheriff. Same place as Todd Stevens.

He was on his back, the EMT s trying to revive
him, but it didn't look like they stood much chance.
The deputy was taking pictures, and the dogcatcher
was loading two dogs into the cages on his truck.

Two Akitas.

I recognized one of them because Musashi had
bred her last year. She was a beautiful dog and
threw some great pups. I walked over to the truck.

"What happened?" I asked.

"Who are you?" the dog warden demanded.

"I know one of those dogs," I said, pointing to
the cage.

"You the owner?" He was taking out a pad of
forms.

"No. I just know one of them."

"Who owns it?"

"Kate Wilhelm. Lives up that street."

I pointed to Lakeview Drive, just around the lake. "What happened?" I asked again.

"It looks like these two of man's best friends ran that guy to death. This Wilhelm's in a lot of trouble."

I looked at Todd. The EMTs had given up and covered his body. The cop was talking on his radio. He looked up when I walked past.

"Who are you? What are you doing here? We don't need any sightseers right now."

"I'm Hank Eston. I was supposed to meet that man at his office. When he didn't show up I came looking for him."

"How did you know where to look?"

"His secretary told me he'd gone jogging at the lake.

"Can you ID him?"

"Yeah. He's Todd Stevens. He runs the Holistic Health Center on Highway 73. I don't know him well, but I know him. Knew him."

The deputy was giving me a long, hard stare. Great. Here we go again.

"Stick around," he said, "and don't get in the way."

I walked over to talk to the EMTs, but they couldn't or wouldn't tell me anything, so I wandered around with my hands in my pockets, looking at the lake, the trees, the ground. It was still damp from yesterday's rain, and I could see Todd's footprints leading to his body. I could see two sets of dog prints, too. I followed them back quite a distance from the ambulance scene, studying them carefully. They crossed each other and Todd's tracks. I sat on my haunches and thought about what I saw. Then I went back to take care of what I had to with the deputy. He was taking more pictures of Todd.

When I finished with the deputy I went back to the HHC to do two things: get the package Todd had left for me, and to warn Serene that she might be promoted. She gave me the package. I didn't tell her he was dead, just hauled off in an ambulance. I left a check made out to Todd Stevens for fifty dollars and filled out the memo line with ''for two grams of *lu chiao*.'' I'd have to put the fifty back in the account, but I wanted some sort of record.

Now there was no choice but to go see Riley, before my name turned up again on his desk and he had me hauled down to Silvern in a patrol car. There was no more chance of enlisting the aid of

Amos Johns and doing it by remote control. I gave him a quick call.

"Amos, all this is getting complicated. Listen, if the cops ask you about that day on the hill, just tell them straight, okay?"

"Sure, son. Why not? When you comin' to see me?"

"How's Tuesday, if they don't lock me up?"

"Tuesday'd be fine. Call before you come."

"I will. See you then, if I can." As soon as I'd hung up I remembered the cattle were coming Tuesday. Damn it.

FIFTEEN

I DROVE TO the Madison County jail and went through the initiation ceremony again, got a green badge this time, but was escorted to the same room, with the same stench and, I swear, the same popcorn on the floor, to wait for Riley. There must be a decent room, somewhere in the place. It had to be Riley's doing.

"So you come home to roost." Riley arrived with another deputy. "What are you doing here, besides saving us the trouble of arresting you?"

"For what?" I asked, taken a little by surprise.

"For what." Riley smiled a mean "I gotcha" smile.

"Skip it. I got something for you," I said, sure of my ground.

I reached into my jacket and pulled out the package from Todd's desk and threw it on the table. I saw out of the corner of my eye the deputy behind me was a little nervous. I'd moved too fast again, but I was annoyed at Riley and didn't pay it any mind. I knew I was right.

"Go ahead, open it."

Riley opened the plastic sandwich bag of gray powder.

"What is it?"

"I got that from Todd Stevens today. I bet that's what Bill Evans was involved with. That's why he was killed, and I think I can tell you some of the people responsible for his death. I was hoping to give you Stevens, but I guess you've got him anyway, now."

Riley didn't say anything for a minute.

"So what's your point?"

"My point is, get off me. I didn't have anything to do with Bill's death. He was involved with a poaching ring that sold deer antlers for use in herbal medicine. They're the ones who killed him. I know that someone at North Cottonwood Freight was involved. They used the trucks to haul the stuff down to the airport, where they shipped it to an outfit called Eastern Rim Enterprises. Todd Stevens was a middleman for them on local sales. I've only got one other name for sure, Mike Carson, one of the poachers.

"I'm going to give you the method, the opportunity, and the motive. Bill was beaten so severely that it killed him. He met with his attackers on Sunday night. He'd found religion and wouldn't be involved with anything illegal anymore. They were afraid he'd spill it to you or to Game and Fish"

Riley chuckled. "That's good, you shit. That's real good. Now let me lay something out for you, wiseass. Two guys get killed. What do they have in common? They're both balling Sue Fenton. Who gives a shit who's balling Sue Fenton? Hank Eston. He's jealous, he wants her back. He beats one guy to death and sics a pair of dogs on the other."

"Wait a minute. You think I killed Stevens?" I couldn't believe this shit.

I got control of myself and thought things out a little. I smiled at Riley. He got angry.

"McCauley," he said. "Frisk this clown, then go down to the dispatcher's records and bring me the tape they're holding for me. Oh, and take that bag down to the lab and get them to find out what's in it." McCauley frisked me, took the bag, and left.

"So you're tying me into two murders instead of one now, is that it?"

I was still smiling. Riley wanted to erase my smile by removing my teeth, but I was reasonably sure he wouldn't. I had an ace.

"There's nothing concrete to tie me to Bill's death."

No answer, just a glare.

"Because there can't be anything. I didn't do it."

I still had a little faith in the system. Not much, but a little. I don't know why.

"That leaves Stevens's death, right?" I pressed.

Still no answer. McCauley came back with a portable tape recorder and one cassette. Riley set it on the table and put in the tape. McCauley left again.

"How about two murders and an assault charge?" He punched the play button and we listened to me calling for the ambulance for Amos.

"Chickened out, didn't you? Didn't want to see Amos Johns die too, so you called for help, but you didn't stick around. Don't you know we record every, and I mean every, incoming call here?"

I had suspected as much, but I didn't know they kept them, and I sure didn't think they'd cross-reference them by voice. Riley must have taken a personal dislike to me. Or maybe it was his idea of a thorough job.

"I made that call, but I was fighting for Amos, not against him. I asked him to keep me out of it because your guys were already giving me such a hard time. He'll testify to that."

"The hell he will."

"If it ever comes to it, he will. He's an honest man."

He shot me a look that said he'd never heard one guy in there say that about another.

"Your deputy at the Stevens scene was taking pictures. Do you have the prints back yet?"

"No, not yet."

"When you get them, take a close look at them"

"Listen, wiseacre, don't tell me what to do. Stevens got run down by those dogs and—"

"They never touched him," I interrupted.

"They ran him until he died. That's still going to be murder."

"Get those photos and a *Peterson's Field Guide to Animal Tracks*. I'll show you why you're wrong."

Riley glared a few seconds, then left the room. I heard the lock go home again. I was on my second cigarette when Riley came back, carrying a field guide and a manila file folder.

"You can't smoke in here. County ordinance. Put it out."

We could have argued about misinterpreting laws, but instead, I pulled a quarter from my pocket, stubbed the cigarette out on it and put the butt back in the pack. Riley looked surprised. I hate butts on a floor. Anybody's floor.

Riley spread out some photos and gave me the field guide.

"I had these faxed in to us. Now show me."

I opened the guide to the section covering dogs, tracks running and walking. I gave him the book.

"Look at the tracks in the pictures. Those dogs weren't running hard. They would have had him a long way back if they were. And an Akita could snap your leg if it wanted to. They were just loping and walking along with Stevens. See how the tracks in the photos are doubled up here? They only overlap when the dog's walking or at most slow jogging, not running full out. Check the book."

He did.

"You're right," he said.

"Akitas can be made mean, but they're not naturally, and that female never seemed mean to me when I was around her. The dogs tagged along for the exercise and fun."

Riley looked at me in silence, reevaluating. He heaved a sigh, rubbed his eyes.

There was a knock on the door. McCauley stuck his head in.

"That stuff in the bag was powdered antlers, probably from mule deer," he said.

"Thanks," Riley said, without looking up. When he did he looked a little brighter.

"So how did you come to be in possession of an illegal substance?" he asked.

"I bought it from Stevens just before he died. I figured it would prove he was dealing in the stuff, that you could bust him for that and get him to tell you the names of the guys in the poaching gang and shut them down. And then, maybe, get one of them to admit to Bill's murder. I know that's blown now, with Stevens's death, but you should still be able to track these guys down."

He stared at me, eyes gone tired and, I'd almost have said, sad. He closed them and rubbed them again, slumping back down onto his elbows.

"Look," I said, "the autopsy will show what killed Stevens. He lived out of balance, trying to slim down now and then to keep the girls after him, but not really taking care of himself. He was taking his secretary's Nardil, and he'd just had a heavy lunch with cheese and beer. He must have been nuts to go jogging after a meal like that."

"Yeah, yeah," he said, not looking up. "Just leave the detecting to us and the medical analysis to the coroner. Get the fuck out."

"Out?"

"Go. Just go."

I got up and went to the door quietly.

"Eston?"

"Yeah?"

He was still leaning on his elbows, pinching the space between his eyes.

"Thanks for that bit about the dogs," he said. "I would have missed that."

I walked out of Riley's dungeon, out of the jail-house, with mixed feelings. I was relieved to have the county off my back and to be done with the whole mess, but something about Riley was still bothering me. I wondered if I would ever find out why he'd been so hard on my ass.

SIXTEEN

I'D LIED TO Jim Geist about having the squeeze chute ready, so when I woke Tuesday I realized I'd have to get up faster than I really like to. Breakfast would be essential with the kind of day I had ahead, and the chute did have to be oiled.

Jim had been running herds on the ranch for several years. I maintained the fences and gear and salt blocks and generally kept after the critters while they were grazing. He did the buying and selling of the ninety or so head we ran each summer, and paid my uncle pasture rent at sixties prices. I owned twenty of the steers, and we split the costs and profits proportionately. He got good grass cheap and I got the profits off twenty cows. It wouldn't have paid to run that few alone, and I didn't have the bucks to run more. I guess I could borrow the money, but when you go into debt you give up your freedom. I prefer to live on a cash basis. It also gave us a way to keep Luke Sigilli out of trouble two days a year, although I always thought having him work with us was about the worst part of it.

I checked the squeeze chute and oiled everything up, then put the hundred-pound propane bottle and gas burner next to it for heating branding irons. I double-checked that the sweep gate and squeeze chute were aligned properly so we could maneuver the cattle off the truck and down the inclined backing chute into the holding pen. Then we'd use the sweep gate to guide them one at a time into the squeeze chute, a device that consists basically of two vertical panels of welded bars, much like old jail cell doors, that can be forced together to immobilize a cow while you brand him, castrate him, and give him his inoculations against disease.

Jim would be up with the cattle in the next hour or so, Herefords or Hereford crosses, I hoped. Jim always looked for a bargain, but generally stayed with Herefords. They cost a little more, but they put on good weight and have minimal health problems.

The semis arrived, two of them, following Jim and Luke in Jim's Jeep. The day's work got started.

We heated the branding irons and laid out a supply of syringes and drugs on the bench kept near the squeeze chute. Luke manned the gates, huffing and puffing with the weight of an unnecessary

Frontier .44 strapped on, while Jim did the cutting
and I did the shots and branding. I never could castrate a bull without getting a twinge below the belt.
Branding is a little cruel, but done properly, not too
deep, it isn't that painful, and a brand can't be cut
off like an ear tag can be, if a cow breaks through
a fence and meets up with someone lacking in hon-
esty. A cow represents a pretty good chunk of change.

I put salve on the brands. Jim disinfected the
cuts, and we opened the squeeze and let them out
one at a time into a twenty-acre pasture, where the
newly-steered steers could spend the night with
hay. That way I could keep an eye on them to be
sure no one got sick or swelled up too much.

It was a long day. A hard and dirty day with just
a lunch break and quick breaks for water. My chaps
got another layer of crud on them and I did too. I
let Jim keep the oysters. That belt thing again.

After Jim and Luke left I sat up with the critters
for a while, having a smoke and watching to see
that none of them got sick or crazy. Well into twilight I heaved myself up and went home for a bath
and dinner. One problem with living alone: when
you're dog tired, the bath seems like an imposition
between dinner and bed. I made do with cold reach-
ins and a beer, took a quick shower, and collapsed.

Next morning I saddled one of the horses, took the dog with me so he could get in a little run, and opened the gate from the twenty-acre holding pasture onto the main place. The cattle had already formed into roughly three cliques, each with one or two leaders. The leaders eyed me while the followers stayed back slightly. One took a few nervous glances around me, then began a slow but rapidly accelerating sneak through the gate. It turned into something of a stampede, like shoppers at a K Mart blue-light special. Once past the gate, everyone stopped running and milled around. No one knew exactly what to do with their newly purchased gadgets.

I guess the first thing a person does with freedom is to test the boundaries and look for weak spots in the constraints. Cattle do the same. One of the leaders began walking south along the fence. The Moose and I followed along, holding off about fifty yards so as not to spook them, just to be sure the fences were okay and no cattle broke through. And to bring them back in if they did. Unless they run short of grass, cattle don't usually push through a fence after the second day on a place, but I don't fully relax about it for a week or so. Young cows have the firm belief that wherever they can force their heads to go their bodies can follow. That includes through a fence. Occasionally during the learning process one gets stuck in a fence, or even in the fork of a tree. It's unbelievable.

These yearly cruises always put me in a mind to reflect on cows and people, all of us looking for greener pastures, filling our faces and emptying our bowels as we go, finally settling for whatever we get. The whole process of raising cattle for slaughter used to bother me. So much death. Then I turned it around and looked at so much life instead. Butchering an animal you've killed yourself, whether having raised it for meat or hunted it in the wild, puts you right in the middle of good questions. The connections of one species to another. The animal's life and death. Your own. It's come close to a religious experience for me at times, with glimpses of purpose and dignity in a cycle that seems perfectly right. Everything in this world is food sometime for something else. Trying to deny that cycle is like trying not to breathe. It violates nature.

One of the leaders, a dun-colored fellow with an eye canted a bit skyward, stopped and turned around to see what I was thinking. I reined in the horse, who looked a moment at Cant-eye, then lowered his head to browse. Musashi sat, tilted his head, and looked at him too.

"Poor dumb bastard," I told him. "One season

of this nice life for you, and then it's down to the concentration camps.''

The horror comes in when it's put on a mass scale at a slaughterhouse. The questions raised there can't have any good answers. Any sense of purpose or dignity in the end of an individual life are stripped away in the stench and the gore of industrial-strength efficiency. You see it in the faces of the workers in the packing plant, especially the killers. Not only cattle die there.

Anytime anyone eats a commercially packed steak or hamburger, he becomes a part of something ugly. Hell, I'm a part of it myself. I brand and castrate and feed and doctor these guys to no other purpose than to send them to die and get packed and rendered for meat and glue and leather. I eat supermarket meat and use Elmer's and wear boots and chaps and gloves and belts.

''If we didn't, you wouldn't even be here, ol' Cant-eye. There wouldn't be any cows at all. At least you get a summer of fresh air.''

He snorted, turned, trotted a few yards, and then dropped his nose to the grass. Well, I hadn't found it all that convincing either, but I was beginning to identify uncomfortably with his lot in life.

''No one lives without someone dying,'' I yelled after him. ''Not even you. Elk and deer and gophers and rabbits catch hell on the roads and get shot and even poisoned so you can eat that grass. You vegetarians ain't a damned bit better!''

Thinking of vegetarians made me think of Sue, and Sue made me think of Bill. Death again. Murder. Killed not for food, but maybe so someone could have more to eat, more territory to graze, more something, even if it was just for a moment.

"Even if you don't kill, somebody dies," I muttered.

Cant-eye got moving again, feeling lonely I guess. The other cows and the Moose and the horse and I finished our three-mile jog around a half section of land. Back at the cabin I unsaddled the horse and turned him out with his buddy. He shook his mane as if he'd never had to listen to so much nonsense in his life. Musashi and I went inside for lunch.

AFTER SOME FOOD and a nap I saddled the gelding, tying my saddlebags on behind the cantle. It was getting near to sunset, but I wanted to make sure of the fencing on a pasture I planned to open up for the cows in the morning. I got my fence pliers and work gloves from the truck, a few pieces of splicing wire wrapped in leather, and my yellow rod fence-stretching tool from the barn and loaded them up. I got my rifle in its scabbard from the house, let the dog out to trot along, and mounted up.

The Moose and I went along leisurely, checking the fence, watching the cattle, and keeping an eye out for stray dogs. New neighbors are constantly moving in and out now that the area has become a suburb, and they usually take awhile to realize they can't just let their dogs run loose. They gang up and chase, sometimes attack, livestock and wild game. Usually one warning shot placed just over their heads or just beside them will teach dogs not to come back.

I didn't see any dogs, but I did find one broken wire on the fence. I dismounted, took out a splice wire and my stretcher and gloves, and began patching it. Probably an elk had jumped the line and didn't jump quite high enough. No big deal. Musashi wandered away from me, down into a slight draw. My horse stood off about ten yards, his reins dragging the ground as he grazed. I had both ends of the broken wire locked into the yellow rod and pulled together ready for a western-union splice when I saw that the strand had been cut, not broken. Then a bullet spattered dirt beside me. I was on my way to the ground before my brain registered the report. I rolled over to the horse, jumped, and grabbed my rifle, then slapped his rump to get him out of the way. It was a damned good thing I took my hunting horse. The mare was gun-shy and I'd have been unarmed.

I yelled to Musashi to stay in the draw as I ran in a crouch, zigzagging back to a tree near the break in the fence to lie prone. I looked over the ground on the other side. A slight slope of open grass ran to a line of trees three hundred yards out, then dropped into a valley. Nothing moved. No sound but the wind. I scanned the tree line and on my second sweep I spotted someone behind a big fir. I levered a .308 cartridge into my Model 99 Savage and took aim. I intended to knock the bark off the tree and tell him to give up when he took off at a run down into the valley. I put a shot into the ground behind him to hurry him along and keep him from thinking about having another try. All I saw as he ran was that he was a good-sized guy, dark-haired and maybe a beard, in brown clothes.

I waited about ten minutes, keeping my eyes open, then figured to hell with it; I couldn't sit there forever. I put the rifle's safety on and rolled away from the fence and down toward the Moose, where my horse was standing. The draw was deep enough to give a little cover, so I used it to mount up and get out of there. The splice could wait for another day.

When I got home I unloaded the rifle, put the horse in the barn, and ran to the house. I called Riley in Silvern and told him what had happened.

"Did you get a good look at him?"

"At three hundred yards? Hell no," I said.

"Then what do you expect me to do? We can't do much without something to go on. Did you see his car? Did you get a license number?"

I kept silent a moment, running through my mind what was possible. Not much, really, but it was Riley's attitude that was getting to me.

"You know, shooting across someone's property without permission is against the law. You got your neighbor's permission?" Riley said.

"Me? What about the guy that took a shot at me?"

"Ah, but you shot when he was running away, when the immediate danger was over. That's a no-no."

"I wanted to let him know I'd return fire," I said. "It seemed important to do something to defend myself before he improved his aim. Besides, if I'd been aiming at him, we'd be able to identify him. He'd still be there."

"Well, if your neighbor doesn't press charges against you, I guess we'll just let it go. This time."

"I doubt that the National Forest is going to

complain. Aren't you even going to send out a man to pick up the bullet that missed me? We can dig it out, I'm sure.''

''Chain of evidence is broken. No witnesses and we don't have a gun to check it against anyhow. No harm done, was there? You didn't get hit, right?''

''Yeah, no harm done,'' I said sarcastically. ''When do you guys decide to do any work?''

''Our motto is 'Nil sine Numine,' nothing without providence.''

I'd always thought the county motto meant nothing without a number. In a way Riley was right, there wasn't much likelihood of catching the guy, but you'd think an attempted murder would elicit some response from the law. Maybe if it hadn't been me.

What bothered me most was having it happen *after* I'd been to the cops. That bothered me a lot.

SEVENTEEN

I STUCK TO THE ranch for the next couple of weeks, keeping an eye on the cattle and packing a six-gun and carbine everywhere, just like Luke Sigilli, keeping the other eye on the rim of the trees. I read the weekly valley rag, hoping to see that the cops had sewn up the poaching gang and Eastern Rim Enterprises, if not Billy's murder. Nothing.

An old friend called to invite me to a Midsummer's Eve party in Cottonwood. In the dead of winter there's Christmas. We've abandoned the old Teutonic rites of winter solstice and turned it into our own colorful celebration to take the edge off the doldrums. When summertime rolls around in Cottonwood some of us try to revive Midsummernight's Eve. We fail, of course, virgins being hard to come by in Cottonwood, but we make do. Maybe the Calvinists are right and everyone should be working the extra hours of daylight. Maybe my friend is right and they should party all night.

I cleaned out my truck cab, at least down to the seat covers, put on my dress boots and jeans, took my best hat off the steer horns above the door, and went into Cottonwood.

The party was in full swing when I arrived, beer and wine, hot dogs on the grill and people of all sorts inside and around a backyard pavilion. A portable tape deck was putting out Mexican music to provide a background rhythm for conversation. It was a closed circle this time around, no new faces, but I had a few beers and talked with a lot of people I hadn't seen in a while. Everybody was very earnest and intense. I overheard swatches of the holistic litanies "kidney," "liver," and "gall bladder" so many times that it was a relief to catch someone lecturing on scarcity as nothing but a state of mind. Not much was news. Not much is when you live in a small town in modern times. I didn't want to talk about the trouble I'd been messing with. I was there to enjoy myself.

I left just before ten, alone as usual, and drove down off Forest Heights to head home. When I stopped before turning onto 73 to look for traffic I saw a white van, North Cottonwood Freight written on the side, pulling into Granite Way.

None of the last month's events had made much difference to them. None of the month's events had gotten any law enforcement agency to do anything either. After all the crap I'd been through. After laying it on a plate in front of Riley and being told to leave the detecting to them. God flat damn it.

It wasn't a problem I was outfitted for that night, but it sure as hell looked like it was my problem. I drove home fuming, but planning.

Step one in the morning was to remount the snow plow on the truck. After that I rolled out the four showy, wide chrome wheels and tires that had been on my truck when I bought it and swapped them for the narrower tires I keep on it to get good traction in the snow. I napped and loafed the rest of that day and the next, playing with the dog and enjoying the advantages of being independently broke.

About eight p.m. I checked the truck to be sure it was full of oil and gas and tried the plow one more time, to be certain everything worked right. I loaded ten ninety-pound bags of concrete mix from the storage shed into the back of my truck for extra weight. I'd return them before I needed them to set wooden fence posts. I taped red-and-black For Sale signs on the tailgate to allay the suspicion of anyone wondering what a snowplow was doing on the road this time of year. I put a fake phone number on them, just in case someone had a good memory, and smeared the license plates with manure. They'd remember the phone number, not the plates. I taped a For Sale sign on the plow, too. Then I drove through Cottonwood and out to the interstate to wait in the dark for the van from the freight company that operated only in the daytime.

I pulled off the road, parked perpendicular to traffic. My truck looked like just another junker parked so people could see it was up for sale.

On schedule, at 11:15, the van drove past. I raised my plow and fired the engine to follow. Up a hill I kept pace. Then came three miles of flat and I caught up. Past the captive, relatively tame buffalo herd and the award-winning scenic overpass that's scenic only in the other direction. But I wasn't watching the view, just the van about two hundred feet ahead, keeping one eye out for police cars. We passed the flashing sign that warns trucks of the seven-mile, 6 $\frac{1}{2}$ percent grade. I closed the gap to a hundred feet. The van sped up a little. We headed down the hill at sixty in a fifty-five-mile-an-hour zone. No traffic at that hour, no cops in sight. I knew they hang out at the top and bottom of the hill, not the middle. We passed the sign for the runaway-truck ramp. In one mile there'd be a half-mile lane of soft gravel ending in water-filled drums, set out to stop a truck gone out of control, and a concrete barrier wall on the right to keep the truck from going over the side, two hundred feet to the canyon floor below. The van sped up to seventy. I pulled out to the middle lane, coming alongside it. The driver looked over to see what kind of crazy I was. He had dark hair and a beard. I thought I recognized the SOB who'd taken a shot at me twice now. I hadn't been expecting to combine pleasure with work.

He must have recognized me, because he tried to back off and get behind me. I expected that and hit the brakes. He sped up then, trying to outrun me. Which is what I'd planned for him to do. We were even with the runoff ramp. I paced him, angled my snowplow to the right so only it would make contact, not the truck itself, and raised the blade all the way up. I goosed it and turned into him. He tried to steer out of it, but that's why I had the extra weight in back. I pushed him into the gravel and kept pushing to the right until he was riding the concrete wall. Sparks and shrieks came from abrading metal peeling off the van's side. It slowed. The gravel was doing its job. I pulled the transfer case lever back to throw the truck into four-wheel drive so I could maneuver when we came to a stop. The van, with two-wheel drive, would be stuck in the gravel.

A very scared driver tried to open his door. The passenger side was stuck shut against the concrete. I pushed the control lever and angled the plow to the left, creasing his driver's door shut permanently. The glass shattered and fell out. I backed the truck up three feet, grabbed the log chain that stays under my seat, and pushed my door open.

The driver was trying to climb out of the broken window, but he was just big enough to give me the time I needed. It was Blackbeard. He had to be Don Lorenz.

I ran and put two loops of chain around his neck, then looked for something to cinch it to. There was a grab bar behind the door, to help get into the cab. I made use of it for another purpose, pulled the chain tight through and around it a couple of turns, then hooked it. Both ends. His head was pulled tight against the door frame. He might get loose, but I doubted it would be before the State Patrol got there to help him. I reached in and grabbed his hair.

"You know, this is going to cost you that fancy black bike of yours," I said.

"It ain't mine. It's Wilhelm's."

"Wilhelm's? The Wilhelms are in this?"

"I'm just the gofer. He's the boss, not me."

"The fucking Wilhelms are running a poaching ring? Upright, respectable, Republican Wilhelms?"

I cut myself off. Their connections could explain a number of things if I thought it out, but that could wait for later.

"Hey, let me go, huh, man? What do you say?"

"I say tough shit. I don't like being shot at, ass-hole." I opened the van's rear door, tore open a few of the packages of antlers and flesh addressed to ERE, and left him cursing, a present for Riley.

Then I got the hell out of there. I pulled off the highway at the Morrison exit, went under the in-terstate, and doubled back west on the old highway north of the interstate. Two miles up I pulled into a side road and got out a wrench and a screwdriver, dropped my tailgate, and took off my plow and plow frame. They're heavy, but I knew from ex-perience I could manhandle them if I needed to. I loaded both into the bed of the truck, tearing hell out of the concrete bags, but I got them in, made them look like a load of junk and took the For Sale signs off. The cops might be looking for a truck with a snowplow on it, but not for a pickup hauling scrap iron. They wouldn't figure one man could take off and load up a plow by himself. Judging other people by your own limitations is always a mistake. I wasn't worried about the van driver pos-itively identifying me. It might come out that he'd tried to kill me and that would get him into more trouble. Possibly.

I made it home without a hitch, unloaded the plow, and put it back on the ground, making sure by flashlight that no visible damage had been done. I rubbed off a few patches of white paint, swapped wheels again, and buried the wide chromes in the manure pile. I went in the house and broke out a bottle of stout to celebrate a job better than well done, even if it had cost me a good log chain. When the State Patrol opened the van and found a shipment labeled "plastic parts" that consisted of ground antlers, I knew two and two would come together into four or five for them, and the poaching ring, Bill's killers, would be out of commission. I went to sleep a contented man.

EIGHTEEN

I TURNED THE RADIO ON at breakfast and listened through another inaccurate weather forecast and a fifteen-minute sports segment. I paid attention to the three minutes that covered international and national news and stopped eating when the blurb about an accident at the runaway ramp on I-70 came on. The State Patrol had called in the Sheriff's Department and Game and Fish to arrest the driver on charges of possession of illegally obtained wild game. No mention was made of a second vehicle. I didn't expect one. I smiled, turned the radio off, and finished breakfast.

I was taking it easy, working next to the wood-pile, Musashi snoring nearby, when I heard the sound of an approaching vehicle. I nodded at Moose to answer his questioning look. In the three years we'd been together I'd learned only a few of his body language signals. He'd known all of mine since he was three months old, but then he was just a dog.

Traveling salesmen don't drive this far back on empty dirt roads, and the Jehovah's Witnesses and I had reached a friendly truce years ago. A red Wagoneer crested the hill and rumbled over the cattle guard. Musashi resumed snoring, having performed to the full extent of his duties as far as he was concerned. I got no premonition of danger and figured one of my friends had bought a new car. Maybe someone had finally won the lottery. I leaned on my ax and watched to see who it was. Riley. I couldn't help glancing at my snowplow.

"What are you doing here?" I grunted.

"Can't a guy just drop by?"

"Didn't you see a closed gate and a No Trespassing sign?"

"I saw 'em. I closed the gate and I ain't trespassing. You invited me, remember?"

"I don't. It's not likely, either."

Riley shrugged. "So now that I'm here, don't I get invited in?"

I shrugged. "Come on up." I swept my hand in an "after you" gesture toward the porch.

He turned at the top and said, "Hey, can I offer you a beer?"

"I thought you were on duty"

"Naw, just a social call. Besides, we hot-shot

detectives can get away with a drink now and then.''

"In that case, sure.''

I laid my ax against the pile. I expected Riley to go to his jeep, but he ducked through my open front door and took two beers from the refrigerator.

"Hey!'' I yelled coming up the stairs.

"Hey yourself,'' he said, coming out and holding out an uncapped beer to me. "The guys said they saw a good supply of these in the icebox. You don't want to let this stuff get old and skunked. Salud.'' He took a drink. We sat.

"You didn't drive out here to see the trees,'' I said.

"No, I didn't. I came to tell you that we got the antler business wrapped.''

"About time,'' I said.

He looked down, then out to the peaks.

"Yeah,'' he said. "Well, there was a little more to it.''

"What more could there have been? Between me and Amos, you had everything you could need.''

"Yeah, well, not quite. There was the matter of the Wilhelms.''

"The Wilhelms. Ahh. Finally.''

"Yeah, they were in it. They were the brains and

the money on this side of the Pacific. Owned half of Eastern Rim.''

''Take you a month to uncover that secret?''

''Look, Eston, you got reason to be pissed. Just hear me out, will you?''

''Okay,'' I said. I drank my beer.

He swirled his and finished it, then looked at the refrigerator.

''Another?'' I asked.

''Maybe it should wait till I finish,'' he said. ''You might change your mind.''

''Hell, have a beer.'' I went in and got two more.

''Look. I left the New York department 'cause I couldn't stand this shit. I was young, I could start over. I figured out here with the hills and the cow pies I'd get enough rank fast enough that I wouldn't have to put up with any more of it. But I guess it's everywhere, in the end.''

Riley was having a rough time.

''When Bill Evans turned up dead, word came down to put a lid on it. When you came sailing up right on the scene, it looked like the best way to do that was to hang it on you. That idea looked even better when Takayama took such an interest in the autopsy report. What with the girl's testimony that he'd said he'd been beaten up, there wasn't any way just to sweep it up in the lab.

"Then, when Stevens bought it, the same noise came down the same track, only even louder. I was supposed to bust you then and there, evidence or no, lock you up, and drag it out as long as it took to nail you. But when Stevens's cause of death turned out to be a stroke caused by all that shit in his system, Nardil, Furoxone, booze, some other crap, I was right between a rock and the hardest place. Especially since I'd let you go. The coroner called it death by accidental drug abuse. The pressure was on him, too."

The name Furoxone started ringing in my head, but I didn't want to mention it.

"So why'd you let me go?"

"Because it stinks. It still stinks. I knew you didn't do it, do either one of them, and I knew you didn't have anything to do with the antler bit.

"For a month now, the Evans case has sat with no work on it, nowhere to start. The antler thing is a joke to everybody but State Wildlife. Nothing would ever have happened out of the Sheriff's Department on that one if it hadn't been for that incident on I-seventy last night. No way to keep that one covered, even if it had been one of our guys instead of the state that got the beef."

I fought back a grin.

"I came out here to say I'm sorry. It just stinks

when a clean guy gets caught in that shit. It stinks when anyone's caught in it, but for us I guess it's a way of life.''

''So who was sending the word down to nail me?''

''Forget it. You can't touch it. There's no paper trail, nothing. It was done to protect the Wilhelms and ERE. I got to live here and work here, too old to start over again. So I ain't about to do a damn thing about it. I let you out of there last time you were in. That's going to make promotions tough for a long time. That's it. That's all. No more.''

We sat for a while, not looking at each other. At the moment both of us thought Riley was pretty ugly and that Pike's Peak looked pretty good. I thought it through a few more times. Riley wasn't the whole problem, just part of it, but without the Rileys in the world just following orders and doing their jobs, corruption wouldn't work. Maybe Riley deserved a place in hell, and maybe it takes a whole lot more courage to stand and fight than Riley had in him. You can't blame an elk for eating your garden, and I couldn't fully blame Riley for coming up short. That didn't mean I liked him or appreciated his part in what'd happened, but I understood.

''Hey, Riley,'' I said. ''Let's get rid of two more of these beers.''

It took him a minute, but he nodded and smiled.

NINETEEN

IN THE MORNING I drove over to see Kells. I wanted to tell him the whole tale, of course, but mainly I wanted to establish an alibi for the night before last. Riley's glances at the snowplow probably hadn't meant anything, but I believe in CYA.

It was warm and still, with a few clouds floating toward Denver. As I rumbled down his drive I could see him on his lower, varnished redwood deck, practicing with the sword. I parked, closed the truck's door quietly, and tip-toed out along the upper deck to where I could watch him.

He was dressed in black, the top similar to a karate *gi*, but instead of baggy pants he wore a pleated, split skirt called a *hakama*. The *kata* consisted of long periods of sitting on his heels, followed by flashes of the sword. When he cut two-handed the blade whistled like an arrow in flight. At the end of each sequence the sword would flash into the sheath faster than the eye could follow. All but the last foot or so; that went in as slowly as you set down a valuable china cup with too much tea in it. There was something eerie about his concentration, not like a dancer's or someone reading.

Finally he drew the sheathed sword out of his belt, laid it gently on the deck, and bowed deeply to it from a sitting position. Then he picked it up very slowly, stood, and bowed to the massive stone outcrop to the west.

"Eston-*san, ohayo gozaimasu,*" he said. "Good morning. Come on down."

I went down the outside stairs to the lower deck. He ushered me into his studio through sliding glass doors. We sat on the floor under a wooden Buddha placed on a varnished redwood windowsill.

Even though I'd done the remodeling for him, the room seemed strange to me. While most of his house smelled of tobacco smoke and furniture polish, this room smelled of incense. We'd glassed the whole north wall, but there was still a cavernous feel to it, faintly exotic and mysterious.

I told him all of it while he cleaned his sword. When I mentioned Sue's uncle having preached the gospel while he was raping her, he nodded and muttered something.

"Pardon?" I asked.

"That might account for it," he said.

I let that go by, not remotely understanding it.

"Any chance I could have been having dinner with you here night before last?" I asked him. "Riley came over yesterday evening and paid some attention to my snowplow."

"The beef was great, wasn't it?" he grinned. "Loved that bottle of red you brought. I'll ring Monika in a minute and remind her to thank you too."

"Thanks."

"Look, I'm sorry, but I have a problem or two with the way things have been put to rest."

"Like what?"

"I'd rather not say, yet. Why don't I bring a six-pack, since your rancher friend said he likes his beer, and we'll pay him a visit. I'd like to ask him a few questions."

"Okay. I'll call and make sure he'll be there, then we can go."

"Great. Thanks."

Amos was home and said he'd enjoy the visit. Kells changed and we drove the forty minutes without saying much. It was a glorious, sunny day, heating up a bit. It looked as if the rains might be over for a while.

Amos was mucking stalls when we showed up. I held up the beer and he was delighted. He stuck his pitchfork in the pile, smiled, and shook his head slowly. He pulled off his gloves and walked out of the barn. We each took a beer and leaned against the side of my truck. I introduced Kells.

"The doc says I shouldn't, what with my medication," Amos said, holding his bottle up to the sun, "but you're only young once. Here's to you, son."

I lifted my bottle to him and we drank.

"Funny thing about that kidney. I still don't recall getting hit in the back during the whole fracas, but then I was pretty busy at the time."

"Me, too," I said.

"But I do recall feeling a little stitch back there," he rubbed his back, "when Miss Susie was giving me a treatment that morning. Just before we met." He took another drink of beer. "Maybe the old back is getting what they call psychic."

"How long have you been going to Sue?" Kells asked.

"Just once. Pulled a muscle and the doc recommended her. It helped a lot."

"Did you get to know her much?"

"No, just about my back, and that weird business about the horoscope. Don't hold with that kind of thing, but I told her my birthdate and place and all, just to keep her happy. Ding-a-ling blonde. I tried to console her in her grief, told her how Jesus had helped Bill and suggested she might give Him a try. She got all tense when I started quoting scripture. Fact is, that's when she missed a stroke or something in my back, so I shut up and quit distracting her. She's a nice girl, actually started crying when I told her. A little nutty though, don't you think? Hand me another beer.''

"So she hadn't made up your horoscope before she worked on you?" Kells asked.

"No, sure hadn't. Think that made a difference?"

"I'm sure it did."

"You believe in that stuff?"

Kells shrugged.

We talked through the second beers. Kells, a doctrinaire Zen Buddhist, showed what seemed to me to be superb restraint, listening to Amos on the subject of his church. He paid polite attention, nodding and smiling and even asking an occasional question, but to me he seemed somehow far away.

We said good-byes and climbed into the truck. When we'd driven half a mile or so, out of sight in a stand of pines, but still on Amos's land, Kells asked me to stop.

"A few things we should discuss," he said.

"Okay," I said. "Shoot."

"Were you able to find out what kind of system Sue practices?"

"Yeah. It's on her business card." I pulled out my wallet and gave it to him.

"Ah," he said, looking at it. "Of course. Studied in New Jersey under Chow, or one of his disciples. And did you find out who her kung fu teacher is?"

"She said Ling. Sifu Ling."

"Ling. Damn it, I was afraid of that. Right. One more question. You read Stevens's obituary in the paper?"

"Sure. I was surprised at the age they gave. I thought he was a lot younger."

"I expect everyone did," he said. "He was probably lying about it out of vanity, and was handsome enough to get away with it."

"So what?"

"So it falsified his horoscope."

"And that means what?"

"Look, he claimed he was born in 1957. I know that, because that's the year Sue had on his chart, the Year of the Yin-Fire Cock. But he was really born in 1945, the Year of the Yin-Wood Cock. In a New Age community like Cottonwood's, you have to be consistent with the branch, or Animal Year, in Chinese astrology, but almost nobody knows the stems, only serious students, like Sue.

Twelve years' difference, you see. Same day, probably the same place and hour, but off *exactly* twelve
years.''

"Okay, okay. So what the hell has all that got to
do with antler poaching?''

"Not a bloody thing.''

We sat there silently for a full minute, Kells staring stiffly through the windshield. Something was
weird. Too weird. The beers were wearing off, leaving me to my own devices. Those devices were
battered to hell by Riley, the cows, the sniper, the
hairy scene on I-70. And I'd pretty well had it with
the mysterious East.

"Aren't we done with this?'' I asked irritably.

"Hardly,'' he snapped.

"What is it with you? What the hell piece of it
are you chewing on? It sounds as if you've got an
ax to grind.''

He didn't answer, just kept staring straight ahead.
Images floated through my tired mind, of Kells with
his sword, with his library in Chinese and Japanese,
the Buddhas and incense and bells and gongs. Of
the strange moment between him and Sue that my
Jesus rant had caused in the Pines. Of the relation-
ship between him and Diane Meyer, so close that
his permission had to come before she'd tell me
what the powder was. Of his story of deer ranches

in Japan. There was someone behind the antler racket, someone with connections in the East. And I never did know what Kells did for a living. All I knew was that he flew out of Denver a lot, and did some work for a company in Kyoto.

"Just exactly where does your money come from?" I asked.

"What money?" he asked back, still staring.

"Seriously, damn it. Tell me."

He stiffened. A moment or two later he drew a big breath, let it out loudly, then drew another.

"There is a mode of understanding, a set of ideals and instructions of enormous value buried in the past of China and Japan. A way of seeing and knowing past anything in the West since the desert fathers and the alchemists. We've turned our backs on all of that, actually burning or starving anyone who has shown any interest in it. Now the only hope for any of that saving us from the horrors into which we've driven ourselves is to revive that way of seeing and knowing.

"So I teach. I teach by first trying to teach the teacher to be someone worth listening to. By learning all I can about these vestiges of wisdom and finding ways to convince gum-chewing California surfers and paranoid Chicago suburbanites who dream of taking out Mike Tysons with one magic kick-punch that karate isn't the point. I fly to San Diego or San Francisco or Chicago or Cleveland and spend a weekend trying to do the impossible. Trying to bring something more important than TVs and Toyotas across the Pacific.''

Suddenly he pushed the door open, jumped out of the truck, and slammed it closed again. He paced a circle, bent now, almost shuffle-footed, muttering. He stopped, raising his head to face me through the window. He looked a sick, worn sixty instead of the healthy forty-five or fifty he had looked a few minutes ago.

''That's what I do. I've written a little about how I do it, and so have come to the attention of one or two Japanese cultural groups who want to do the impossible, too. Not Sony or Mitsubishi, I assure you.''

He turned his back on me then and stumbled off a few paces, really bent now and clutching at his back under his jacket, rubbing. He stopped and after a while straightened and turned back to face me. He walked back to the truck like an officer in a funeral parade, opened the door, sat down, and resumed staring out the windshield.

''I don't make any more in an average year than you do,'' he said at last. ''I live off my wife's salary, her sweetness, her sweat. I do not deal in mutilated wildlife, and I am no more a murderer than anyone else who pays taxes and eats beef.''

We sat in embarrassed silence. After awhile he pulled out his Dunhills and offered me one. I took it.

TWENTY

I REMEMBER DREAMS only occasionally, usually if I'm camped out. When I woke the next morning I knew I'd had a rotten one, but none of it stuck in my memory.

Musashi washed my face when I came down from the loft, but I rinsed it in the sink anyway before I started coffee. My mind was numbed, not wanting to join my body in the morning rituals. I figured breakfast would help.

Something nagged. Furoxone? I'd known about the Nardil, of course, but why Furoxone? Sue had a bottle of it. Maybe it was common enough for residents of Cottonwood to have *Giardia* that I'd meet two who'd had it prescribed.

Slab bacon and homemade bread, two eggs, and a pot of coffee returned me to the feeling of satisfaction I'd gotten out of forcing Riley to bust the antler poachers, a satisfaction only slightly marred by the knowledge that he'd probably never nail them for Bill's murder. Still, I knew they'd done it. Maybe I could nail them someday.

It's hard to be clear about why I did the next thing I did. Maybe I felt like I'd won a joust and wanted to collect my wreath from the lady. Maybe it's hard to live with a triumph all by yourself. Or maybe it was just gonads again. I picked up the phone and dialed Sue's number.

"Hello?"

"Sue. Can I come over? I want to share something with you."

"What?"

"It's about Bill. I think I've got the whole story now."

"Ah, I don't know."

"Come on, Sue, it'll help you get over the whole thing."

"Oh dear. Oh dear sweet..."

There was a long silence, then a long sigh, then another silence, time enough for me to wish I hadn't made the call.

"All right," she said at last.

"I'll be over in a little while." I called the Moose in and left.

Sue had a pot of tea ready when I arrived and I took a cup, with honey, and one of the muffins she brought from the kitchen. I walked to her herb collection and held up her bottle of *tu chiao shuang*.

"This, Sue, was the ultimate cause."

She let out a deep breath and collapsed into a chair.

"Wow," she said.

"Bill's biker friends were poaching deer. Stevens was the middleman, locally, on sales, and Bill was using freight company trucks to deliver the powdered antlers to the airport. They were shipping it overseas, a big operation. It was the poachers who beat Bill up, not the guys at the trucking company, when he wanted out of it. I'm convinced of that. And a little auto crash the other night got the cops off their duff to round up the whole crew. A relief, huh?"

"Yeah, a big relief to me. I didn't know," she said.

Something was worrying her. Maybe thinking about Bill's death. Maybe avenging it and bringing the culprits to justice didn't matter to her as much as it did to me. I couldn't help it. I was disappointed.

I returned the *lu chiao* to the shelf, then noticed Sue's vial of Furoxone. I picked it up and idly counted the pills. There were only three left. I looked at Sue.

"Put them down, Hank," she said in an icy voice. She shook her head and pinched her nose.

"Hank, would you excuse me? I'm getting a terrible headache. Why don't you come back later? Give me a couple of hours to lie down, will you, Hank? All right?"

"Sure."

She arched her back, pushing the outline of her nipples through her gauze dashiki, and made an attempt at a smile. "I'll give you my most sensuous massage."

"Sounds great," I said, but warning bells were going off all through me.

I left and drove down from Piñon Trail to the library. I found a *Physicians' Desk Reference* and looked up Furoxone.

What the guy at the pharmacy had told me over the phone had been true as far as it went, but there was a lot more to it. The contraindications were serious business. No alcohol for at least four days after the last dose. Nothing containing the amino acid tyramine or monoamine oxidase inhibitors, MAOI. No yeast products. No ripe cheeses, no beer, no antidepressants like Nardil. Mixing those with Furoxone would lead to a hypertensive crisis, probably with muscle cramps, especially in the legs. What it amounted to was that it would put someone's blood pressure through the top of his head. Literally. Cerebral hemorrhage. I closed the book slowly and returned it to the shelf.

I wasn't sure why, but I decided to call Kells. He answered and I told him what I'd found.

"Did you count the remaining pills?" he asked.

"There were only three left."

"And she didn't invite you for a meal?"

"No, she didn't."

"Then she's going to try it the other way," he said. "Did she ask you to come today, or was it your idea?"

"My idea."

"Good, that improves our chances a bit. Look, Eston, don't go back there for at least an hour, not until I get there. I've got to get a few things organized. Go to the Pines and wait for me. Have...let me see. I don't know what you should have. Have a salad and a glass of wine. That's just a guess, but it should be all right."

"What's going on, Brian?" I protested. "I want an explanation."

"Do it, damn it. Just do it. I'll be there as fast as I can."

HALF AN HOUR LATER, Kells and Diane Meyer entered the Pines and came to my table, where I was sitting in front of the remains of a dinner salad and an empty wine glass, sipping coffee and having a cigarette. Meyer arranged her huge purse on the fourth chair and they sat.

"The coffee's bad," she said to Kells. Then to me, "How much have you had?"

"This much," I said, pointing to the half-empty cup.

"No more. It may not be too bad."

"All right, what's this about?" I asked Kells. "I understand about the Furoxone and Stevens, but what's all this?"

The waitress came over and asked what they wanted. Meyer ordered an herb tea. He ordered coffee. Not too considerate. We sat in silence until the waitress had cleared my place and come back with their cups. Kells leaned forward then, close to my ear.

"She's going to try to kill you, Eston," he said softly.

"Not with Furoxone, she's not."

"Right, not with Furoxone. She's going to try to kill you the same way she killed Billy Evans."

"Billy Evans? She didn't kill him, Carson and Lorenz and those guys did."

"I'm afraid not. But if that's what you believe, then I can only ask you to go through with my plan to indulge me. If you're right, it will clear her of all suspicion."

"Who suspects her?"

"I do."

It all sounded like pure bullshit to me. I couldn't imagine what had led him to such a conclusion.

"So what's this plan of yours?" I asked.

Kells and Meyer exchanged glances. Hers said it was up to him.

"What I want you to do is go up there and let her give you that massage. Diane and I will conceal ourselves where we can watch her doing it. That means you'll have to keep the curtains open in the main room. And the door unlocked."

"You mean you want to watch her giving me the massage, without her knowing you're watching. Why?"

Kells sighed, pulled out his Dunhills, glanced again at Meyer, and put them down.

"Listen. They tell you that all this New Age, Oriental, holistic health treatment can only help you, can't do any harm. In most cases that's true. It can't hurt much because the practitioners don't understand it well enough for it to help much, either. They haven't enough power to make it work either way. Also, a lot of it is derived from simple folk medicine, which has a history of helping and not hurting.

"The Chinese stuff is different, though. Acupuncture, Chinese herbals, *t'sui na* massage, all derive from the same science as *t'ai chi*, kung fu, *pa kua*—the fighting arts in general—and all the other Chinese sciences, from astronomy to building fortifications. It's all of a piece, like nuclear power without the waste. It can be used to blow Hiroshima or cure cancer.

"The point is, Sue studies both *t'sui na* massage and a particularly deep form of kung fu. Both. Both systems are based on the *wu hsing* system. They use the same pressure points, the same meridians. Touch them one way and they'll cure sclerosis of the liver. Touch them another way, and they'll hemorrhage the kidney."

So that was it. I pictured Bill's body. There'd been hardly anything, three bruises. The marks on his face had been no worse than if he'd slipped out of a chair and hit something sharp or rough. Still…

"Still," I said, "I can't believe Sue has that stuff down well enough to have that much effect. More like what you were saying before, not enough power. She's a space queen, into horoscopes and actinic rays. Come on, Kells."

"You heard Johns tell you about her missing a

stroke, didn't you? And neither of you remember him taking a blow to the back, do you?"

"Yes but—"

"You said you saw a bruise on Stevens's back just after she'd been working on him, didn't you?"

"Yeah, but Stevens died of a stroke, probably brought on by mixing Furoxone and Nardil with cheese and beer. Sue may have put that stuff in him, but that's something else. And Amos is still alive and kicking."

"All right," he said. "You don't have to believe it."

"You want me to be one of your wildlife experiments?"

Kells blinked slowly and lit a cigarette, thinking. I felt my face go red.

"Justice, Eston. I thought you were interested in truth and justice and all that?" he asked.

I nodded my head. "I am."

"Then help me. Just go through the motions with us, will you? A little experiment. A little adventure, hmm?"

I got a Dunhill out of the pack and let Diane Meyer wrinkle her nose all she wanted. The way Kells put it, if Sue wanted to take a whack at me while I was on the massage table, or if she was going to try to kill me some other way, they'd be there to cover. She had a reason, I had to admit. I knew about the Furoxone. It was probably down the toilet by now, but I did know about it. I wasn't sure who I could trust or who had their heads on straight, but like Kells said, a little experiment, a little adventure.

"Okay," I said. "Okay, what time is it?"

"A little after two," Meyer told me.

"Let's do it."

TWENTY-ONE

I EASED MY TRUCK up to some aspen and brush that would conceal them within a few yards of the window of the main room, where Sue's massage table was set up. There was just enough slope there for them to see in. I watched them go toward the far side of the grove until they were out of sight, waited what I thought was long enough for them to get into position, then drove up and knocked on the door.

She was dressed in a short, red silk robe with gold dragons on it, barefoot, as usual. She said "Hank" in a breathy voice and came up to kiss me. I was too tense to respond, and embarrassed, knowing Kells and Meyer were watching.

"I'm so sorry about funking out earlier," she breathed. "Let me make up for it now."

She led me by the hand to the massage table, leaned me against it and started working on my buttons. I fumbled to help. She left me to my shirt and went for my belt.

I remembered another reason I'd split with her. She liked undressing me, and I hate the awkwardness of being undressed by someone else. I put up with it until it was time to get at the boots and socks. There's no way to get jeans off oversize twelves. I hung on to my jockeys. With people watching there was no way I wanted my ass completely in the wind.

"Face down to start," she whispered. "We'll get some kinks out of those great shoulders." Sue had a way with flattery.

She worked the muscles of my shoulders and the back of my neck. Velvety, all velvet. I found myself drifting a little, beginning to wonder if I hadn't been wrong to leave her back then, if everything might not have smoothed out if I'd stayed on. Everything so smooth, so velvety.

"I'm moving down now to the shoulder blade," she murmured. "Very tight there. I may have to dig in a little."

I said something like "Mmm." I didn't want to talk. No wonder massage is catching on. Who wouldn't want to be rubbed this way?

I felt a thumb go under my left shoulder blade, digging in a bit. It felt good. Then I felt another hand smoothing my back, down past my jockeys, down to the right thigh. Just above the knee I felt a pinch, with a knuckle, maybe, and the soft part of the thumb. Then the hand above let go of the shoulder blade and moved down around the upper lumbar, and pinched, too. That one didn't feel as good. There was a buzzing sensation running through my buttocks and down to where she was pinching my knee. I didn't like that. The buzzing started to extend from there up the other way, back into the shoulder blade. I could feel her pinching the knee harder. The buzz was turning into paralysis. I tried to call her name, to tell her to stop, but nothing came out. I felt her hands drop away, but that didn't stop the buzzing. Then I heard her scream, the sort of high, keening shout you hear sometimes in karate classes, and then she struck my right kidney a blow that carried a kind of sick pain I'd never even imagined.

I was writhing with it, making a sound I didn't know was in me. Through the red in my eyes and the ringing in my ears I became aware that Kells was in the room, tangling with Sue, although I couldn't make out just how that was going. I heard Diane Meyer speaking to me softly, felt her holding my head from above and gently massaging behind my ears.

"Be still, Hank. You must be still."

I was on my back at that point, but she got me

to roll over prone again. She was digging something out of her purse. I couldn't stop writhing. Bile was rising into my throat.

"You must be still, Hank. Hold still, just for a minute."

I spat, accepted the idea as a challenge, and held still. I could feel the acupuncture needles going in, setting up new patterns of buzzing.

"Just a little longer, Hank. Another half a minute. Hold on."

I held on. Three, maybe four more needles. The buzzing pattern shifted.

"Brian," Meyer said, "is she under control?"

I could hear Sue sobbing. "Yes," came Kells's voice. "Enough."

"Can you bring me Hank's chart from the wall?" she asked him.

"Yes. It may take a moment."

He dragged Sue past my field of vision, holding her wrists together in one hand. His face was bleeding. I didn't get to see Sue's. He reached up and tore down one of the horoscopes, presumably mine, and brought it over to Meyer.

"Damn," she said. Then after a moment, "Well, not too bad."

She let the chart fall to the floor. It landed right under my nose. I watched the characters spin around the circle for a while. The buzzing wasn't so much like buzzing now as it was humming.

"Two more needles, Hank," she said. "You're doing great."

I guess I was. The pain was nearly gone. There was just the humming among the needles, like the power in high-tension cables. I started drifting again.

"How long will you have to leave them in?" Kells asked her. He had moved with Sue into my line of sight again, had put her in a chair and knelt looking at her, very calm and straight-backed.

"Another ten minutes."

"Right. Sue, we know how. Why? Why Billy?"

She kept her head down, staring at her hands folded in her lap. She was swinging her head from side to side, then rocking back and forth from the waist. I was glad I couldn't see her face.

"What the hell did you do that for, Sue?" I yelled. "You're supposed to be my friend."

"It was an accident," she said.

"Aw, bullshit!" I started to get up, but Diane's hand pushed me back.

"I never meant to hurt him."

I realized Sue wasn't talking about me, but about Bill Evans. I shut up.

"But ever since that damned Amos converted

him he couldn't shut up about Jesus. I was giving him a massage when he started in. I couldn't stand it. It was like roaring in my ears, a blinding black form pressing me down, hurting, hurting..."

Her voice was softer after that.

"I disappeared. Just went away. When I came back, he was on the floor, unconscious. He'd cut his face on the wheel lock of the table.

"I guess I half-knew then what I'd done, but it wasn't real at all. I got him onto the sofa. He was breathing, but roughly. I fell asleep. I couldn't face it. I fell asleep. He stirred once sometime during the night. I petted his face. Then I slept again. When I woke in the morning he was dead."

"What about Amos?" Kells asked her.

"I never thought he'd come to me as a patient. It was sudden. He started in on the same Jesus stuff. I did it to him a little too early. It didn't work."

"Too early?"

"Before it became roaring. Before the black came down and the hurting."

"And you didn't have his horoscope."

"I got it later, though," she said. Her voice was rough again, almost gloating. Then the soft tone returned, sad, regretful. "I had Billy's, though."

"Why didn't it work on Stevens?" Kells pressed her.

"He lied. He lied about the stem, you see, the heavenly stem. So even though the day was right and the time and everything, it couldn't work because he'd lied about the stem."

"I doubt if it would have worked anyway," Kells told her. "You didn't have the roaring, or the black coming down."

She looked up curiously, like a student questioning a teacher who had just tossed out a fast one. "You think that was what made it work?"

Kells held her hands together. "It traces back to your Uncle George, Sue. What do you think?" he asked Diane.

"The charts help," she said. "Perhaps in the strict practice of her system, they would be essential. Generally, though, none of these techniques work very well unless you're in an almost trance-like state. It could work only if both criteria were met."

"Why Stevens?" Kells went on.

"He wanted to ruin me. Didi and her damned sun sign predictions about people near me getting hurt. Amos Johns and his damned 'She missed a stroke.' There are no secrets around HHC, in this whole mean town. I had to stop him."

"So, knowing about his hypertension and that he

was taking Nardil, you came up with the idea of mixing Furoxone into his special lunch.''

''*Giardia* is so common up here in the mountains that when I called my doctor to tell her I had a dose, she prescribed it by phone. She told me all the warnings. It wasn't anything I'd have to worry about, since I don't drink or take antidepressants, but I knew I could make it deadly for Todd.''

''I guess you'd better call Riley,'' I said.

''Not Riley. I'll call Takayama. Riley'd never believe it,'' Kells said.

''Shouldn't I get to a doctor?'' I asked.

''You're being treated now by one of the best,'' he said. ''What's the prognosis, Diane?''

''I got the needles in fast enough, and the horoscope was a great help,'' she told him. ''He'll be feisty as ever in two days. Probably won't even bleed.''

I figured I'd reserve the right to consult an MD.

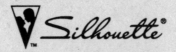